MW01196580

Doug Fletcher book 3
Dean L. Hovey

Print Isbns
Amazon Print 978-0-2286-1292-6
B&N Print 978-0-2286-1293-3
LSI Print 978-0-2286-1294-0

BWL Publishing Inc.

Books we love to write ...
Authors around the world.
http://bwlpublishing.ca

Dedication

To Fran Arms Brozo and Anne Telker Flagge

There are a number of people who help me take my rough manuscript and turn it into the finished book and their assistance is invaluable.

Thank you, Jude Pittman and Susan Davis, of BWL for your guidance and support.

Julie Hovey comments on early drafts and helps with the medical situations and terminology.

Fran Brozo has become my muse, offering support when I'm discouraged and ideas when I've written myself into a corner.

Anne Flagge read early versions of the manuscript, suggested improvements, and proofread later versions.

There are dozens and dozens of fans who've kept me energized and enthused.

On August 26, 2017, the eye of Hurricane Harvey hit Texas, crossing uninhabited San Jose and Matagorda Islands before hitting the town of Rockport where it destroyed every apartment building, condominium, and hotel. A few miles south of the hurricane's eye, Corpus Christi, Port Aransas, Mustang Island, and North Padre Island were subjected to westerly hurricane-force winds that battered and deluged them with rain. In an August 2019 interview, the second anniversary of the hurricane, the mayor of Rockport said he hoped the city would be "substantially" rebuilt in another 3-5 years.

Chapter 1

Ted Kaplan walked into his suburban Minnetonka mini-mansion after a lengthy day of trial preparation. He set his briefcase and computer bag inside the door, loosened his tie, and slipped off his shoes. He hung his suit coat in the closet and looked for his wife, then remembered she'd flown to Texas to inspect their newly rehabbed Mustang Island condo. After pouring two inches of Scotch into a low-ball glass, he sank into a recliner and leaned his head back. The trial was the culmination of a three-year investigation into a drug, human trafficking, and prostitution ring. It would be a media circus but would provide invaluable media exposure and name recognition for him. The convictions, a foregone conclusion, could pave his way to a political or judicial appointment. The pressure to nail down every detail and script every word of his opening comments was immense.

It was after eight o'clock, and the fall twilight lingered over the lake and across his manicured lawn. He grabbed the remote and clicked through the on-screen guide until he found ESPN. The Minnesota Twins were in the playoffs, and he'd missed the game but hoped to find a game recap. His eyes drifted to the framed pictures over the fireplace. He and Wendy had been photographed at dozens of fundraisers, smiling alongside politicians, civic leaders, the rich, the famous; all the right people to move his career ahead. He had a brief pang of regret. Wendy pointed out the pictures were missing children. They'd fought before she'd left, and he'd conceded that their biological clocks were ticking. It might be time for her to stop taking birth control pills. His future now seemed secure, and she could forgo a few charitable board meetings to create time to be a mother. Early in their marriage, there had been hints from both sets of parents about grandchildren, and later came quiet questions about their ability to have children. Following that came hints about in vitro fertilization. The latest bombshell was a suggestion they get on an adoption waiting list, dropped by his sister at his nephew's birthday party.

The Scotch was half gone, and he was deciding between fried rice or pizza leftovers when the doorbell rang. He set the glass on a coaster and walked to the door in his stocking feet. He checked the security camera and saw a man in a uniform standing on the front step holding an envelope. In the background, he saw the white Kwik'n Ezee Delivery van. He wondered if his paralegal had found something he needed to see before morning.

"I have a package for Theodore Kaplan that requires a signature." The deliveryman held out a white sheet on a clipboard and pointed to the next blank line on the sheet. Kaplan smiled. If he'd been a superstitious man, he would have been concerned his was the thirteenth signature on the sheet. He signed, and the deliveryman handed him a small padded envelope.

After closing the door, Kaplan ripped open the envelope and removed the computer thumb drive. He checked the outside of the envelope, but there wasn't a return address. He shook it, expecting a hand-written note from the office or packing list. Empty. He took his laptop computer out of the briefcase, inserted the thumb drive and finished the Scotch while it booted up. A momentary flash of the MPEG file title flicked on the screen as the computer loaded, and then a video clip started to play. He poured more Scotch and watched idly at the pornographic image of a couple having sex, the quality obviously filmed by an amateur. There was no sound other than muffled sexual noises and an indistinct crash of waves washing against a shore. He'd watched hours of video from the sting operations, but this was more pornographic. He expected the Marshals to burst into the scene at any moment.

He stopped the video and searched the envelope again. His mind raced, determining if the video might have to do with the case he was prepping for trial. If this was intended for the trial, there would've been a chain of evidence tag or a note indicating the video was a copy and explaining the context.

He restarted the video, expecting to recognize the man as one of the trial defendants. The poor camera angle showed the man's naked back and grinding hips. He looked at the surroundings in the bedroom, thinking those might give him some hint of the location. His focus locked on a seascape mounted over the head of the bed. He studied the bedside tables, the phone, the alarm clock, and froze. The scene was the bedroom of his own Texas condo. When the man arched his back, Ted saw Wendy's face. Her hair was matted, make-up smeared, and she looked dazed.

He moved to turn off the video when he noticed the time stamp in the corner of the frame. The footage had been filmed that morning. Wendy Kaplan had flown to Texas the previous day. The man turned his head, showing his face to the camera, obviously unconcerned that he would be recognized.

Kaplan slammed the laptop lid, picked up his cellphone, and hit the speed dial number for their Port Aransas condo. The phone rang five times before rolling over to the answering machine. "This is Wendy and Ted. We can't come to the phone. Please leave a message." The phone beeped.

"Wendy, are you there? Pick up the phone." Kaplan hung up the phone and stared at the laptop. His hand still rested on his cellphone when it rang.

The caller I.D. said, "TheoKaplan."

"Ted, you tried to call the condo, but Wendy is...indisposed right now. If you want to see her again, you'd better get here before she's strung out too long."

"Listen, you sonofabitch, if you..."

"I hear rehab programs are less effective the longer the user's been on heroin. In case you're thinking about calling the cops, well, opioid overdoses have become the scourge of our society. If the police respond, they won't find Wendy in time to administer a dose of Narcan, especially with all the Fentanyl-laced heroin on the street these days. Do you understand me?"

"Yes."

"Sadly, there aren't any direct flights between Minneapolis and Corpus Christi. You can connect through Dallas. That'll get you into Corpus Christi early tomorrow. Or, you can book a redeye flight to San Antonio and drive down yet tonight. It doesn't really matter, because you'll be in Texas Monday morning which will make you unavailable for opening arguments."

Kaplan ran his fingers through his hair as his mind raced through possible solutions. "That'll just delay the trial if that's your objective."

"Not if you disappear with the opening comments, the case files, and your personal notes." The caller paused. "There's a very discreet treatment center on Grenada specializing in heroin addiction. By the time Wendy finishes her treatment, and you return to Minneapolis, the case will be dismissed, and I'll be long gone."

"There might be a delay, but someone else in the office will step in and try the case."

"But they're not Ted Kaplan, the golden boy with the golden tongue, and they'll be in disarray without your files, notes, and opening statement. You don't really think any of the other young, overworked, underpaid assistant county attorneys will be able to equal the performance of *the* Ted Kaplan, do you?"

"They'll track me down."

"Not with your new passports. Plane tickets and a limo will be waiting when you show up at the condo. You'll be traveling as Mr. and Mrs. Eric Johnson."

Before Kaplan could respond, he heard the dial tone.

He opened the MPEG again and looked around the room shown in the video. His eyes came to rest on the nightstand. A piece of surgical tubing, a spoon, a lighter, and a cotton ball sat out—the tools to prep a dose of heroin. He couldn't see needle tracks in Wendy's arm, but they were undoubtedly there.

Kaplan started to dial the county attorney's cellphone, then stopped. They had Wendy and would undoubtedly have the condo under surveillance. If there were any sign of the police or FBI, Wendy would be dead. He pulled up the American Airlines website and booked himself on a Dallas redeye flight and raced up the stairs, throwing a few items into a carryon bag. He tapped the Uber app on his phone. By the time he'd loaded his notes, the case files, and his laptop into his carryon, the Uber driver was in the driveway.

Chapter 2

Doug Fletcher - San Antonio

After solving the mystery of an extra body recovered from the Wupatki National Monument flash flood, I'd gone out to dinner with the Park Superintendent, Jill Rickowski. She'd pleaded her case for me to stay in Flagstaff as a law enforcement ranger. I told her I was excited about moving to a new Park Service Investigator job in Texas. There'd been a kiss after dinner, leading to a night together. Neither of us was interested in a one-night stand, so I'd convinced Jill to join me for a few days in Texas to sort out our fledgling relationship.

We toured the Alamo, the San Antonio Museum of Art, and the World's Fair Plaza during the day. We spent the evenings eating leisurely dinners in restaurants with live entertainment along the San Antonio Riverwalk and nights in our hotel room acting like newlyweds.

We walked along the river holding hands our last night in San Antonio, watching the young soldiers and airmen with their girlfriends.

She took a step back and looked into my eyes. "We've never said the L-word."

I pulled her out of the flow of people on the sidewalk and into an alcove under a bridge. "I said I loved you while you were sleeping."

"I wasn't sleeping. I didn't want to put you on the spot in case our night in your bed turned out to be a one-night stand."

"Are we past that now?"

She took my hand and squeezed it. "Past what?"

"Past the question about whether Flagstaff was a one-night stand?"

"We're up to a five-night fling now. I think we're now at the point where the novelty is about to wear off, and we'll start irritating each other."

"Have I started to irritate you?"

"Not yet." She pulled me back into the flow of people walking along the river. "Am I irritating you?"

"No, but this place makes the world seem far away. It's kind of like Disney World for adults. I'm almost afraid to leave the magic kingdom in the morning."

"Tell me about your Port Aransas townhouse."

"It's a rental a couple blocks off the main highway and a couple blocks from the beach. It has two bedrooms and two bathrooms upstairs, with a kitchen, living room, and dining room downstairs. The whole interior was redone aft Hurricane Harvey."

"What happens to me in Port Aransas?" The confidence I'd always heard in her voice was gone, replaced with a touch of anxiety.

"You're not asking what happens to you. You're asking what happens to us."

"I guess so."

"Is there anything to keep you in Flagstaff?"

"After the dust settles, I might have some sort of a job in Flagstaff. I might not be the superintendent, but I doubt they'd fire me. I can't see myself sitting on your Texas townhouse deck reading *Home Beautiful* and having supper ready when you walk in the door."

"Before we left Flagstaff, you asked if I could be happy in a relationship with a woman six years older. I think you know the answer to that question."

"Do I?"

I pulled her close and kissed her, blocking the sidewalk. "If you're not convinced yet, I'm not sure there's anything more I can say or do."

She noticed the people backing up behind us. She pulled me into the stream of people and walked quietly, staring at the passing barges loaded with tourists.

"We're both damaged goods," she said as we approached the bridge that crossed over the river in front of our hotel. "Your divorce and my rodeo fiancé left us bruised and wary. I'm a hard-driving type A personality, and you're...not."

15

"I'm a cynical ex-cop."

"Can those personalities mesh?"

I opened the hotel door, and we walked across the lobby to the elevators. Jill gave me a funny look, concerned I hadn't answered her question. We rode the elevator with two other couples and got off on our floor. I closed the hotel room door and led her to the balcony. We watched people below on the Riverwalk. The sound of a Mariachi band filled the evening air. I put my arm around her, but she slipped away and glared at me.

"Are you going to answer my question?"

"We've bared our bodies and souls to each other, and now we've spent five days together that seem to have gone pretty well."

"Those are all the fun parts of a relationship. We haven't gotten into the serious parts. Do you pick up your underwear? Who cooks and who washes dishes? Do you leave the toilet seat up? It's not like either of us is going to change at this point in our lives, and we need to find the 'warts' that'll drive each other nuts. Maybe I should fly back to Flagstaff and not waste our time."

I pulled her close. "Garrison Keillor told a story about a Norwegian spinster librarian who lived with her father. A nice gentleman asked her out for supper and a movie. The father stayed up until his daughter came home and asked her how the date had gone. In glowing terms, she described the man, the meal, the movie, their walk home, and his gentle goodnight kiss. Her father asked if she was going out with the man again, and she replied, 'I don't think so.' Her father asked, 'Why not?' She replied, 'Because it makes the rest of my life seem so sad.'"

Jill pushed back and looked into my eyes. "Are you saying I'm the spinster who's afraid of a relationship."

"I think we both are."

"A week ago, I asked if you could be happy with a tomboy who was six years older. You've never answered."

I pushed a stray lock of hair behind her ear. "If you don't know the answer yet, you'd better come to Texas until you do."

"But the age thing…"

I put my finger to her lips. "I'm more worried about you being willing to accept a divorced, cynical, ex-cop than I am about our age difference."

She pulled away and leaned on the railing. "I'm scared."

"Me, too."

She turned her head. "What are you afraid of?"

"I'm afraid your marriage to your job is stronger than your feelings for me. Move into my Port Aransas condo, at least until you get a call from the Park Service."

"What will that solve?"

"Maybe if I say, 'I love you' enough times you'll start to believe me and agree to stay."

"A few men had said they loved me when all they wanted was to get into my panties."

"You have lovely panties. I can see why they'd make an attempt."

Jill elbowed me. "You know how to kill the mood."

"Hey, I was very careful not to be another jerk who just wanted to bed you. I didn't kiss you the first time we went out for supper because I was afraid of ruining our work relationship."

"You really are a Boy Scout, aren't you? You even offered to turn on an old movie and hold me when I showed up at your townhouse and pulled you into the bedroom."

"I meant it. I didn't want to push you into anything we'd regret. I didn't want you doing the walk of shame as you skulked out my door the next morning."

"You were much more cunning. You became my friend and seemed like you didn't want to get me into bed. I think that's part of the problem—I was the one who dragged you into bed. I've never been entirely sure you were an equally willing partner."

"Wasn't I the guy who kissed you as soon as I found out you weren't my boss?"

She took my hand and led me off the balcony and started unbuttoning my shirt. "It's our last night in San Antonio. Let's see if we can work the magic one more time."

She darted away, scooped a nightgown off the bed, and walked into the bathroom. I undressed and slipped under the sheets. I got the briefest glimpse of her silhouette through the nightgown when she turned off the lamps on her way to bed.

"I think it's funny you don't want me to see you naked after we've slept together for the past week."

"It's not the same," she said, running her fingers through my chest hair.

"Do you have an ugly appendectomy scar?"

"I think it goes back to gym classes. When everyone else's body was developing, I was flat-chested and skinny. And then the rumors started about me being a lesbian, and I just wanted to change out of my gym clothes into street clothes with as few people seeing me as possible."

I ran my hand over her body gently, tracing her muscles and curves with my eyes closed. She squirmed when my finger hit the point of her pelvis. "That tickles." She paused. "Why were your eyes closed?"

"I was memorizing every contour of your body. You could be a model for a sculptor."

"Hoo boy! That's a good one." She pushed herself away from me.

"Sculptors and artists love models with muscle definition and natural curves. You're lovely."

"I have a mirror. I know I've still got a tomboy figure."

"You're definitely a woman."

"You say that like you believe it."

I ran my index finger down her firm abs and slipped it inside the elastic of her panties. She closed her eyes and drew a breath. "There's no question in my mind."

"Shh."

"Are you coming with me to Port Aransas tomorrow?"

"Uh-huh."

Chapter 3

After the hotel brunch, the leisurely drive to Port Aransas took most of Sunday afternoon. We ate tacos at a Mom and Pop place on Mustang Island, bought a few groceries at a convenience store, and dragged our suitcases into the townhouse as the sun set. The townhouse was furnished, but it took a while to find the towels and sheets. By the time we'd made the bed, we were exhausted. I was pleased when Jill claimed a dresser and unloaded her suitcase into drawers. I'd assumed she would live out of her suitcase and somehow claiming a dresser seemed less transient.

* * *

I kissed Jill and left her at the door Monday morning then drove the length of Mustang Island, enjoying the scent of the ocean and marveling at the desert scenery on the west side of the island. At the entrance to Padre Island National Seashore, a young ranger stopped me and looked at my uniform and badge. She appeared to be fifteen years old.

"You're the new guy, Doug Fletcher." She checked a clipboard. "Matt said to tell you his office is in the first building."

I found Matt Mattson, the park superintendent, in the spartan-looking poured-concrete admin building. His door was open, and he was talking with a twenty-something young woman dressed in a green and gray Park Service uniform. She looked like any other ranger except for the pistol on her hip.

I knocked. "Doug Fletcher reporting for duty."

Matt Mattson was in his mid-thirties and wore his hair cropped short, most likely a carry-over from some previous military career. He stood and shook my hand.

"Doug, this is Rachel Randall. Until today, she's been our one law enforcement ranger."

Rachel shook my hand with a firm grip. "Nice to meet you, Doug." Rachel didn't look military or cop-like. Her face was narrow, framed by short dark hair, and she gave off a vibe of someone who was caring. My first impression was that she probably made a great ranger but would be chewed up as a cop on the mean streets of a big city.

"I've been looking forward to having an additional law enforcement person here. Rachel is new, and I've been a little anxious about having her patrolling alone until she gets more experience under her belt. Corpus Christi Police and Nueces County Sheriff's Department are great and always respond when we call for assistance, but they're often half an hour, or more, away."

"Has that been a problem, Rachel?" I asked.

"Not so far, but Matt sends one of the naturalists with me on patrol. I'm going to feel a lot more secure with another law enforcement ranger in the pickup."

"I read your file." Matt motioned for me to take the empty chair next to Rachel. "We've never had a ranger who's actually been a cop." He turned to Rachel and explained, "Doug was a detective in St. Paul, Minnesota after a stint as an MP in a National Guard unit, including one deployment to Iraq."

Rachel smiled. "I'm getting happier all the time. Not only another law enforcement ranger but one who can find his butt with both hands!"

"Doug also knows how to shoot. His file said the last time he qualified in St. Paul, he shot a smiley face on the target in a seven-shot speed trial."

I grimaced. "You could lose that page out of my file."

Matt laughed and Rachel smiled. "That one sentence told me more about you and your pistol qualifications than everything else in the file."

"So, what's the job here?" I asked, moving the conversation ahead.

"Rachel has only been a law enforcement ranger a few weeks. Part of your job is being Rachel's training officer."

"Rachel, what's the job been so far?"

"I patrol the beach south to the Port Mansfield channel and back every morning. Then I walk through the picnic area a couple times mid-day to get after people littering, and then I drive the beach again in the afternoon. Oh, and I've written a couple speeding tickets on the entrance road."

Given the ecological bent of the Park Service, I was surprised about her driving beach patrol regimen. "You can drive on the beach?"

"The sand is hard-packed, so I can drive sixty-miles-an-hour on a lot of it. There are a few soft areas where I have to slow down, but I can usually make it down and back in a few hours."

"I thought you wanted an investigator, Matt?"

"We do." He nodded to Rachel.

"We have people who like to use the beach as a shooting gallery. They show up irregularly, shoot for a while, leave spent cartridges and broken bottles all over the place, then disappear. We regularly get people beachcombing for Spanish coins and also have a few people diving on the wreck of the Nicaragua, and I have to make sure they're not removing any souvenirs."

"Don't you see the shooters coming and going past the gate?"

Matt shook his head. "Not that we know about. Rachel thinks the shooters are boating in across the Laguna Madre, then slipping away. There's also a problem with people using metal detectors trying to find coins. Three Spanish ships ran aground off Padre Island with tons of silver coins aboard. There are still tons of unrecovered coins from the wrecks and a few are found after every storm."

"Is that legal?"

Rachel shook her head. "All of North Padre Island and the offshore areas are an archaeological protection district. It's illegal to use a metal detector in the park, and any recovered coins are supposed to be turned over to a ranger. We get a few turned in a year. I imagine there are hundreds that leave in people's pockets."

"Tell me about the Nicaragua," I said.

"It's sometimes visible from shore, but it's right on the surf line. Most of the people diving on the Nicaragua come from South Padre Island by boat."

"Where's the Nicaragua?"

Rachel got up and walked to a map of the island on Matt's wall. She pointed to a small outcropping more than halfway down the island. "It's an old cargo ship that ran aground in 1912. It carried cotton from Mexico when it got blown ashore on Devil's Elbow during a storm. There are all kinds of rumors about it being a gun and rum runner, but the consensus is it was hauling a legitimate cargo when it ran aground. Other rumors claim it carried supplies for Pancho Villa. That theory is a little hard to swallow since she was steaming north."

"Can you reach it from shore?"

"It's a little offshore just beyond the surf. You can see a little of it above water at low tide. As shipwrecks go, it's not much of an attraction. It's a tough dive because it's right on the surf line, and I guess you get tossed around a lot. Makes it kinda risky because you can get thrown against the hull or some rusty fragment that can bust up your dive gear or break your arm."

"What's the Laguna Madre?"

"It's the channel on the backside of the island," Rachel explained. "It's not a navigable commercial waterway, like Aransas Bay, but there are sport fishermen out there every day."

"Can you see across the island to the Laguna Madre while you're driving the beach?"

"There are a few areas where you can see across to the water, but I can't really get back into the dunes except on foot because the sand is too soft. There are lots of little coves and inlets behind the dunes, and I can't see most of them. I drive about fifty miles of the beach, and people slip in when I'm away from the area where they're shooting. By the time I hear them, or we get a report of gunfire from visitors, they're long gone. We trek back into the dunes and find their debris and tracks, but we've never seen anyone."

"You've been investigating gunfire with an unarmed ranger, Rachel?"

"They're always done shooting before we approach the area."

Matt nodded. "I told her not to be a hero. The shooters are a nuisance, but I don't want anyone to get hurt walking over a dune and getting hit by a stray bullet."

"It's illegal to shoot here, isn't it?" I asked. "It's part of the National Park System."

Matt nodded. "Yes, it's illegal. It'd be the same as shooting in Yosemite."

"Why would people come here to shoot illegally?"

"There are fewer places to shoot than there used to be. A guy used to be able to bring his gun outside the city limits anywhere in Texas and shoot until he ran out of ammo. Now the city limits are spreading, houses popping up in previously undeveloped areas."

Rachel looked at her watch. "If we don't get going, we won't be back in time to check the picnickers at noon."

Matt smiled. "Or you won't be back in time to eat lunch with the other rangers." Rachel's red face gave testament to the truth in Matt's words.

I stopped at Matt's door. "What's the uniform of the day? I wore civvies when I was working in Flagstaff."

"I suppose you should be in uniform if you're patrolling with Rachel, but if you're investigating, you're welcome to wear whatever fits the situation."

"I'll have to find a dry-cleaning shop if I'm going to be on patrol more than a few days."

Rachel looked eager to get going. "There's a dry cleaner in Port Aransas with twenty-four-hour service if you're not into ironing." She stepped out of the office before Matt could offer further comment.

I hung back as she walked away. "I take it Rachel eats lunch with the other rangers daily."

"She was a naturalist before getting her criminology degree and choosing to become a law enforcement ranger. The young rangers eat together and share rumors."

Rachel's footsteps stopped. "Are you coming, Doug?"

I nodded at Matt. "I guess we're off."

* * *

Rachel drove with the surf-packed sand singing under the tires of the Park Service pickup.

I watched out the window facing away from the Gulf of Mexico. "Is all the scenery this boring?"

"Pretty much. The dunes grow and dwindle, and the sea oats grow nearer and further from the shoreline. Aside from an occasional prickly pear cactus, the scenery there on the west side is pretty dull. I've got the swells of surf lapping and receding at the sand on the trip down. Then you'll see the Gulf after we turn around for the return trip. You'll be able to see a few drilling rigs on the horizon too."

"How do you stay awake?"

"I don't know. I just do."

"You make this drive twice a day?"

"Yes."

"The whole way?"

Rachel glanced at me to see if I was kidding. "That's the job."

"You have a lot of character."

She smiled. "What do you mean?"

"This is about the most boring drive I've ever experienced. For you to do this twice a day, without prompting is admirable. It takes personal character to do the good job when no one's watching."

"Thanks."

"What's on the other side of the first row of dunes?"

"It depends on where we are. Mostly there's sand, sea oats, cactus, and scrubby bushes. It's pretty wild like it's been for a thousand years."

"Matt said you were a naturalist. What lives on the island?"

"In terms of animal life, there's mostly rabbits, coyotes, and rattlesnakes in the dunes. Sometimes I see a red-tailed hawk soaring. All kinds of sea life wash ashore, like Portuguese men-of-war, jellyfish, shells, starfish, and sand dollars. I sometimes see tracks from the Kemps-Ridley sea turtles that lay their eggs in the dunes." Rachel's pride in her natural history knowledge was evident in the tone of her voice. She became somber. "I've also seen bottles, pails, rubber gloves, and drums that've washed off boats. Sometimes the sailors dump their waste overboard, so I try to keep people away from anything that looks dangerous or toxic."

"Rattlesnakes?" I asked.

"You don't like snakes?"

"I have no problems with snakes. I was a Scout, and we camped in the wild all the time with snakes. What I don't like is poisonous snakes."

"No rattlesnakes in Minnesota?"

"Not where I hung out."

* * *

We finished our round trip down the seashore in time for Rachel's lunch with the rangers. I located the vending machines and bought a Coke and a bag of Doritos. I found an unoccupied office and put my feet up on an open desk drawer, eating and checking emails on my smartphone. I'd just finished reading a note from Jill saying she'd been shopping and was planning to boil shrimp for dinner when Matt Mattson walked into the office.

"Doug, do you have a second?" He closed the door as he entered.

"Sure, what's up?" I lifted my legs off the drawer, catching my heel and almost tipping over in the chair. I tried to look like it didn't bother me.

"Looks like you're eating the lunch of those who don't know they need to bring a sandwich," he said, sitting in the lone metal guest chair with a cracked vinyl seat.

"I'll have to remember to pack a lunch tomorrow."

"There's a little refrigerator in the break room. Make sure you write your name on whatever you bring. There are rumors that unmarked items are thrown away. It seems the containers are always emptied before they hit the garbage can."

"Rangers stealing food from other rangers. What's the world coming to? Maybe we should put up a security camera in the break room to catch the culprits," I said with a smile.

Matt paused, apparently deciding how to frame his comments. "I need you to be more than Rachel's training officer and listening for people target shooting. We have a problem, and the Park Service Director thinks you're the right person to investigate it. That's why you got this posting."

"You've got my interest. What's going on?"

"I think the shooting Rachel mentioned may be a diversion. The Coast Guard helicopter saw a boat beached on the Laguna Madre side of the island a couple weeks ago. The next day a fisherman reported an oily sheen on the water, and there was a fish kill in the same area in the following days."

"You think someone's been dumping toxic chemicals?"

"There was massive damage here from Hurricane Harvey. Any wooden structure on the islands was leveled. The construction guys have been hauling away tons of scrap building materials every day. Buried in the scrap are hundreds of gallons of automotive chemicals, fertilizer, drain oil, and household cleaning chemicals. Even nastier chemicals, like pesticides, were stored in some of the businesses. The landfills accept the building materials, but it takes special handling and expensive incineration to deal with the chemicals. That means they're a pain to deal with, it costs more to truck them to an incinerator than the landfill, and the incineration costs are much higher than the tipping cost for the landfills. Some of the companies are conscientious and do it right. Others are making lowball bids for rebuilding, and I don't think they can afford proper waste disposal. The landfills are checking every incoming load for liquids, and they reject the loads if they find anything suspicious. That leaves the less conscientious demolition contractors scrambling to dispose of the hazardous materials by other means."

"And you think they may be dumping stuff on Padre Island."

"I know a few of them have been arrested for dumping pails of chemicals overboard in the Gulf and Corpus Christi Bay. The Coast Guard is watching closely. There are fewer places to dump clandestine loads of material onshore because of the amount of development, and the police and sheriff's department are watching every empty lot, and tracing pails and barrels back to the source. So, that leaves the unethical people searching out remote spots to dump their hazardous waste."

"And the backside of Padre Island is remote, undeveloped, and Rachel only patrols the Gulf side of the island."

"Whoever is doing this knows we're spread very thin, and if they drop someone off to shoot up a bunch of shells, they'll distract Rachel, leaving them free to move a half-mile further down the shore where they can toss some pails or drums onshore and maybe throw sand on top of them."

"You're afraid Rachel will get hurt if she investigates." I made it a comment, not a question.

"Doug, she's motivated, but green as grass. I don't think she's prepared to deal with a bunch of folks carrying guns who are willing to illegally dump toxic waste on Federal property. Do you disagree with that assessment?"

"I think it's too soon for me to make that call, but she doesn't have a lot of experience. Do you have a boat or a dune buggy I can use to patrol the Laguna Madre side of the island?"

"The best I can offer is the four-wheel-drive pickups, and they really aren't suited for the soft sand away from the gulf beach."

"How about the Coast Guard?"

"They patrol occasionally, but they've got their hands full monitoring the boats in Corpus Christi Bay and the Gulf."

"Is there a place where I can rent a boat?"

"There are a couple boat rental places where they sell bait. Let me ask around." Matt got up and opened the door. "I might have another option for getting a boat, but I'll have to phone a friend and call in a favor."

"Hey, Matt," I called after him as he walked out the door.

"Yeah?"

"Do you and your wife have supper plans tonight?"

"I'm not aware of anything. Did you want to stop somewhere and get a beer?"

"Jill sent me a text saying she's planning to fix shrimp. I'll ask her to pick up another couple pounds and some beer if you're available for supper."

"That sounds great! We'll bring some Gulf Coast slaw."

"How's Gulf Coast slaw different from other coleslaw?"

"Mandy makes it with minced onion and baby shrimp. What time should we be there?"

"Come over at six."

Matt walked away, and I dialed Jill's cellphone. "Is it okay if I bring some people over for supper?"

"Um, sure. I'll have to pick up some more shrimp, a vegetable, and something for dessert, but I'm out running around anyway. The bigger challenge may be finding pots to cook all that stuff. Who did you invite?"

"I asked the park superintendent, Matt Mattson and his wife over. He said they'd bring

Gulf Coast slaw, I guess it's a local specialty. Oh, and pick up some beer, too."

"I feel so domestic. We're entertaining our first guests as a couple. I may have to buy something to wear."

"I think the Texas dress code is pretty casual. Your shorts, t-shirt, and sandals will be fine."

"Remember, I thought we were staying San Antonio for a few days, and I packed one carryon of clothes. I'm going shopping. You wear what you want, and I'll buy something appropriate for entertaining."

"Whatever."

"What did you say?"

I froze and weighed my words. "I said, 'Whatever you think is best, dear.'"

"You're learning," Jill laughed. Then she became serious. "You do understand I'm kidding. I have no intention of changing you, and I hope you feel the same way about me. I think we fit together pretty well, but it's going to take a while to feel our way around the issue of compromise."

"I learned some magic words long ago."

"Please and thank you?"

I looked around to see if anyone was listening. "'Yes, dear,' covers more situations."

"Now, I'm embarrassed. I'm in line at the liquor store, and people are staring at me because I'm blushing and laughing on the phone. I'll see you at the townhouse, and we'll eat whenever Matt and his wife get there. I'll heat water so it'll only take a couple minutes to boil the shrimp. What time are they coming over?"

"I told Matt to come at six."

"I've got to finish grocery shopping, buy something to wear, pick up the house, change, and prepare dinner. You could've given me a little more warning."

"Yes, dear."

"Stop that!"

"Love you. Bye."

Chapter 4

The aroma of baking bread filled the air as I opened the townhouse door. "You made bread?"

"Don't be silly, the grocery store sells really good 'take and bake' bread. I haven't baked bread since I took home economics in high school. It was one of those things every good South Dakota wife needed to know, back in the '60s. No one actually bakes bread from scratch anymore." Jill wore a flowered blouse, pink shorts, and sandals.

"You look very nice."

"There are all kinds of shops with sales on clothing. I think they were hoping for more tourists than they're getting."

I opened the refrigerator looking for a beer, then saw a cheesecake taking up most of the second shelf. "Who's going to eat all this cheesecake?"

"I met the neighbors, Charlene and Charlie, and they have two boys. I think half a cheesecake would disappear pretty quickly at their house."

The doorbell rang, and I closed the refrigerator. When I opened the door, Matt stood on the steps, wearing a Hawaiian shirt, shorts, and sandals.

"Honey, this is Doug." Matt held a six-pack of Corona beer and two limes. His wife, blonde, trim, tanned, wearing a pink Nike t-shirt, white shorts, and sandals, stood half a head shorter than Matt. I thought, *she's spent hours doing her hair and makeup*. It was tasteful and made her look years younger than Matt. She was a beautiful Southern belle.

"Matt has no manners. I'm Mandy Mattson. Where should I put this bowl of slaw?" She carried a glass bowl covered with Saran wrap containing enough slaw to feed most of the neighborhood. Mandy moved like an athlete, dispelling my initial assumption that she was fragile and dainty.

Jill met us in the entryway, wiping her hands on a kitchen towel. "Please put it on the table next to the butter. I'm Jill."

"I'm sorry. We're a little early." Mandy said with an endearing Texas twang as she set the bowl on the table.

Jill waved off the apology. "You're fine."

"Welcome to Texas." Mandy gave Jill a hug that involved bending at the waist and touching shoulders.

"Thanks. Doug just walked in the door. He needs to change out of his uniform while I heat water for the shrimp."

"Anyone else want a Corona?" Matt held up the six-pack and a pair of limes. "Show me where you keep the bottle opener, paring knife, and cutting board."

"We're still exploring." I slid out the cutting board and got a small knife out of the second drawer I opened. "I think the bottle opener is in the drawer closest to the kitchen table. Open one for me, and I'll take it upstairs while I change."

Jill opened a cupboard and surveyed the glassware. "I bought white zinfandel and pre-mixed margaritas. Would you prefer either of those to a beer, Mandy?"

"I'm a good-old Texas girl who's not much into wine. I'm happy with beer or a margarita."

"No margaritas!" Matt sliced wedges of lime and jammed them into the neck of two Corona bottles, and then added, "Tequila makes her clothes fall off."

Mandy shook her head but was smiling. "Matt, you've got to stop telling people that!"

By the time I changed and got back to the kitchen, hot shrimp drained in a colander, and Matt was on his second beer. Jill and Mandy were shoulder-to-shoulder at the sink, laughing like old friends. Matt stood at the patio door, watching the neighbor's boys wrestle in the yard. He handed me another Corona with a lime wedge sticking out of the neck.

I pushed the lime into the bottle and took a long swallow. "Looks like Mandy and Jill are hitting it off."

"Jill was your boss in Arizona?"

"She moved right from boss to girlfriend."

Matt glanced over his shoulder to see if the women were listening. "Jill's delightful. Most of the people who make it into the upper ranks of the Park Service are type A and have forgotten how to laugh. Jill seems 'alive.'"

"Getting her away from the park has helped. I didn't know she had dimples until after she wasn't my boss anymore."

Matt smiled. "Was that because of the stress you were causing her?"

Jill leaned around the corner. "Yes, it was because of Doug! That's why I have these gray hairs, too!"

"Time to eat." Mandy carried the bowl of steaming shrimp to the table. It looked like enough to feed ten people.

Jill set the basket of sliced French bread in front of Matt. "Everyone dig in."

"How bad was the hurricane damage?" I asked Mandy as I passed the slaw.

"Everything that wasn't concrete was flattened, and lots of concrete buildings had their windows blown out, so the interior walls and contents were soaked."

"Where did you guys go?" Jill asked.

Matt passed the bread and butter. "We went inland, I closed the park two days before the hurricane made landfall. I locked the buildings and told all the rangers to get as far inland as they could before the storm hit. When we came back, it looked like an atomic bomb had gone off. Corpus Christi survived pretty well, but Mustang Island took the brunt of the hit. I think all of the island was covered by a couple feet of water during the peak of the storm."

Jill peeled two shrimp, then got a serving bowl for the shells. "What about your house?"

"It's cement block, like this townhouse, so the structure was still there." Matt peeled shrimp and dunked them in cocktail sauce as he added, "And we'd covered the windows with plywood, but everything inside got soaked, from the carpeting, to cabinets, furniture, and wallboard."

Mandy stopped eating and wiped her fingers on a napkin. "After a day crying while hauling sodden furniture to the curb, Matt had to deal with the park, so I stripped out the carpeting. Our insurance immediately gave us a check to start the repairs, but it was impossible to find building materials, flooring, furniture, or contractors. Everyone was in the same situation. We found a guy to do some of the work while we lived in a trailer parked in the yard. Seven months later we were back in the house. Doug, you're fortunate to have found this townhouse. A lot of the island is still being rebuilt."

"On a happier topic," said Matt, "I've got a friend who's got a boat, and he offered to take us out on the Laguna Madre tomorrow. Would you be interested in joining us, Doug?"

"I thought I was driving the beach with Rachel."

"A guy from the Fish and Wildlife Service offered to take us out. I think we'd better grab the opportunity."

"What's your golf handicap, Jill?" Mandy asked. "You and I can go golfing while the boys are on the water."

"I haven't had a golf club in my hands since I was stationed in Big Bend, Texas, twenty years ago. I'm afraid I'd embarrass myself."

"My friend, Jan, just started golfing this spring. The two of you will be well matched."

"It might be fun, as long as you don't expect me to be Annika Sorenstam."

Mandy laughed. "Oh, Jill, we do it to socialize. Our outings have little to do with making par. I promise Peggy and I won't laugh when you and Jan whiff."

"Doug, we'll pick you up at seven."

"We girls get started a little later. Will nine o'clock work for you, Jill?"

"Nine is fine. What's the dress code?"

"I usually wear a golf shirt and shorts. Tennis shoes will be fine until you figure out if you like golf, and they'll still be fine until you think golf shoes will make you a better golfer. Then, you'll buy golf shoes that won't improve your game, but they'll make you look like you're serious about it."

Jill laughed. "I think I like your attitude."

"You'll like it better after we go to Peg Leg Pete's for lunch."

Matt shook his head. "You're not taking her to Pete's on her first outing, are you?"

"She might as well get the full Mustang Island experience."

"Download the Uber app," Matt laughed. "It'd be bad for the new law enforcement ranger's girlfriend to get a DUI during her first week on the island."

"Ignore him," Mandy said. "Peggy doesn't drink, and she drives everyone home."

* * *

After Matt and Mandy left, Jill scraped dishes, and I loaded the dishwasher. I'd limited myself to the second beer with supper, but Jill had been keeping up with Mandy's margarita consumption, which left the large bottle empty and the two women giddy.

A hand slid up the inside of my thigh, and I banged my head against the top of the dishwasher. "Jeez!" I rubbed my scalp and checked my fingers for blood.

"I'm sorry. Did I surprise you?" Jill gave me her best innocent look.

"Hell, yes, you surprised me," I said too sharply. The hurt in her face made me feel foolish. "I'm sorry. I'm unaccustomed to someone groping me while I'm loading dishes."

"I was trying to be affectionate."

"You're a little drunk." I closed the dishwasher and started the cycle.

"I might have a little buzz." She leaned against me. "It's been a long time since I've felt comfortable letting my hair down around people. I might've had a little more than I usually allow myself. Margaritas slide down like soda pop."

"Mandy was keeping up with your margarita consumption. I think both of you will be hurting tomorrow."

The smile suddenly left Jill's face, and she walked to the stairs. "I think I'll go to bed now."

"I thought you were being affectionate," I said as we climbed the stairs.

"Not tonight. I think I'm going to throw up."

Chapter 5

Kaplan's condo Monday night

"You could've done something besides stand there with your thumb up your butt." Merrill Handy glared at his partner, then looked at Ted Kaplan's body in the bathtub.

Randy "Digger" Dugan shrugged. "Looked like you handled it. I didn't want to get wet."

"Yeah. I handled it and got drenched. Now, we've got to get rid of the body."

"Are we gonna dump him over the railing?"

Merrill wiped his hands and face with a towel. "We're a hundred yards from the ocean. If he went over the railing, someone might see him fall. If not that, someone on the first floor will open their blinds and find a dead guy on their patio in the morning. We need him to disappear for a while. Permanently would be okay too."

"Leave him in the bathtub. The cops will find him in a few days when the neighbors complain about the smell. We'll be long gone."

"We need the Minnesota cops to wonder where he went for more than a couple days. If they find him in the apartment, they'll know who he is and will put the pieces together. If that happens, they'll come looking for us. If someone finds his body somewhere else, but can't identify him, or if he disappears permanently, there won't be questions for a long time."

"Do you have a hungry alligator stashed somewhere?"

Merrill swung his arm toward the patio. "There's the whole Gulf of Mexico full of hungry fish and crabs. If we get the body into a riptide, mother nature will take care of the disposal for us."

"So, we're going to carry him across the dunes and dump him in the ocean?"

"All the condo windows face the Gulf, and too many eyes would see us. We need to carry him out to the parking lot where there aren't any windows, then we'll dump him off the county park pier. The tide will carry him out through the channel, and he'll drift out to sea."

"What about her?" Digger nodded toward the bedroom where Wendy Kaplan lay passed out on the bed. "We only needed her to get Kaplan down here. It costs us money to keep her doped up. Let's dump both of them at the pier."

"I kind of like keeping her around."

"That's because you got to be the porn star. It wasn't as magical for me, running the camera."

"She isn't a problem. She isn't involved in the court case, and she doesn't need to disappear. We can drop her off at a church or a detox center in a few days."

"She's seen us, Merrill."

"She won't remember anything that's happened since we stuck the needle in her arm. She'll be waking up in a bit, let's just see how it goes. Besides, it's going to be hard enough to carry the husband down to the car. It'll look less suspicious if the security camera shows her walking out on her own."

Digger thought about Merrill's comments. Carrying Kaplan's body would be no easy task, and if the woman stopped cooperating . . . "What if she freaks out when she sees him?" Digger pointed to Kaplan's body, still face down in the bathtub.

"We've got to wrap him up, so she doesn't see what's happening. Find some bags or something to put him in."

"Garbage bags? They're not big enough for his whole body, and we've got nothin' to cut him up."

"Then get a rug or a tarp. Find something, so it doesn't look like we're carrying a dead body to the van."

"Why should I be the one to find the rug?" Digger asked. "You find the rug."

"Would you rather clean up this mess and wipe down fingerprints?" Merrill pointed out the havoc created when he'd drowned Ted Kaplan. The towel rack had been ripped from the wall, water was splashed out of the tub and soaked the edge of the bedroom carpeting.

Blood splattered from scratches both made by and inflicted on Kaplan during the struggle marked several bathroom surfaces.

"Oh, Christ," said Digger. "Do you smell that? He must've shit his pants when he died. I'm out of here. I think there's a big rug on the first floor by the elevator. We can use it to wrap him up."

Merrill released the bathtub plug and wiped the blood off the ceramic tile around the tub as the bloody water drained. When he finished, he took a damp washcloth and swabbed down all the bathroom surfaces to remove their fingerprints. He cut the zip ties binding Kaplan's limbs, stripped off his clothes, and ran the shower over his body to wash away the feces and blood. Merrill studied Kaplan's naked body and contemplated the difficulty carrying him to the minivan when he heard keening from the bedroom.

Wendy Kaplan rocked with her arms wrapped around her knees. She looked pale, disheveled, and was letting out a high-pitched whine. Merrill saw the signs of withdrawal and weighed knocking her out again versus just giving her enough heroin to take the edge off her downward spiral but leaving her functioning so she could walk to the minivan. He was drawing liquid into the syringe when he heard the door. Digger walked in with the industrial carpet over his shoulder.

The woman jumped when Digger threw down the rug. "Dude. Every time you give her a hit, there's less to sell. You're keeping her high on *my* profits."

"Just wrap up the husband and stop worrying about *your share* of stuff. Okay?" Merrill got a withering glare from Dugan, but no further argument.

Wendy Kaplan relaxed as the drug flowed into her system.

Dugan watched with disgust. "Are we ready to go?"

"I haven't wiped the living room or kitchen yet."

"I've been gone for like ten minutes. What the hell have you been doing?"

Merrill wiped the syringe and handle of the spoon with the washcloth. "Are you kidding? You saw the mess in the bathroom."

"Wah, wah, wah. Are you done feeling sorry for yourself yet?"

Merrill threw the washcloth at Digger. "Wipe down the kitchen and guest bathroom."

Fifteen minutes later they'd wiped the rest of the apartment, and Ted Kaplan's body was wrapped in the rug. They carried him to the elevator, then across the parking lot to the minivan.

Digger dripped with sweat after loading Ted Kaplan's body into the van. "Let's just leave the woman upstairs. She's out of it now. She'll either wander off, or someone will find her in a day or two."

"We need her to be lost for longer than a day or two. Help me bring her down. The security video needs to look like she's drunk."

"You don't think it'll look like we carried a dead body wrapped in a rug?" Digger followed as they walked away from the minivan.

"Keep your face tilted down. The camera is on the second floor, and it can't get a good angle on our faces."

"Oh, great! Why didn't you tell me that three days ago? It's a little late, don't you think?"

"Just shut up and get in the elevator."

"I think we should dump her with the husband. She's a lot of work, and we're using up product keeping her doped up."

"I told you, I'm not killing her." Merrill pushed the button for Kaplan's floor.

"It won't be a big deal. Just put one of the plastic bags over her head and push her off a pier. You won't be killing her; you'll just be giving her a shove."

Merrill glowered at him as the elevator doors opened. "Just shut up and help me get her downstairs."

Chapter 6

Jill was still sound asleep when I got up, dressed, and brewed coffee. I poured it into an insulated travel cup, went outside to wait. I was taking a swallow when a Jeep towing a medium-sized boat pulled up. Matt got out of the passenger door. A tall thin man met me at the front fender.

"I'm Brad Johnson." The man, dressed like a fishing guide in a quick-drying nylon shirt and pants, offered his hand, calloused and rough. A smile broke across his weathered face.

"Brad's the regional director of the F&WS."

Brad gestured for us to get into his pickup. "We're kind of Federal game wardens. We deal primarily with migratory animals, but we get into other things too."

"I asked him to take us down Laguna Madre," Matt explained.

"Ah, he's your fishing contact."

"We won't be fishing. I'll take you around on an orientation trip. You're welcome to use the boat for a couple weeks if you promise not to sink it or get it shot up."

"I'll do my best to keep it upright and out of the line of fire." Brad glanced at me to see if I was kidding, so I smiled. "I'm a little surprised the F&WS is interested in this or are we towing your personal boat?"

"The fish kill in the Laguna Madre last month caught my interest. The Boston Whaler is a boat we seized during a duck hunting camp raid a couple years ago. We kept it so we would have a boat without all the lights and F&WS logos when we're surveilling someone. By the way, there's a tactical Remington 870 in the portside locker. I assume you've fired a shotgun before."

"One in the chamber and six in the tube," I said with more confidence than I felt. Matt looked lost, so I explained, "It's a seven-shot tactical shotgun. Loaded with buckshot it's as lethal as a machine gun, but only effective at fifty yards or closer. If the bad guys have rifles, a shotgun is not going to save me. If I'm close, that shotgun will give me the advantage."

Brad smiled. "It's loaded with double-ought buckshot. People get very compliant when they're staring at the muzzle of a twelve-gauge shotgun. The locker doesn't really lock, so you need to bring the fishing gear and shotgun inside overnight." He paused. "You have operated a powerboat before, haven't you?"

"Boating is a Minnesota life skill. Although, the twelve-foot Alumacraft rowboat I fished from as a kid is a long way from the Boston Whaler we're towing."

"Same theory, but a couple warnings: If you see a really big wave coming at you, turn into it. If you hear the motor starting to slow, throttle back and tilt it up before you bury the prop in silt. And, don't turn hard when you're going fast, the motor will flip you over."

"Thanks for the warnings."

Brad handed out orange life jackets, each with a USFWS logo, and launched the boat at the Park Service Bird Island Basin. There was no line of vehicles waiting to launch boats, and there were only two other pickups with trailers parked in the lot.

I helped Brad put three fishing rods in rod holders. They stuck up like antennae. "We're actually going to fish?"

"Naw, they're just camouflage."

"I thought the boat launch would be busier," I said as we motored away from the dock.

"Don't even think about launching on the weekend. It's amateur hour. Every fisherman in Corpus Christi will be lined up here, at the county park, or at the ramp under the Kennedy Expressway, waiting for his turn to back a trailer into the water. Half of them will need at least three tries before they get lined up with the ramp and launch their boats."

Once out of Bird Island Basin, Brad opened the throttle, and the boat rose up in the water, racing at a speed that made me uncomfortable. He seemed totally at ease, so I shut up and watched the scenery. The channel was amazingly undeveloped, with most of the shoreline covered with scrubby bushes and prickly pear cactus. Ducks and wading birds flushed from the shallows as we passed. Compared to the crisp gulf breeze, the air in Laguna Madre reeked of decay and stagnant water.

Brad cut southeast, cruising down the channel. The motor was so loud he had to shout to be heard. "This is Laguna Madre. If you stay in the center of the channel, you're not going to hit anything. All the spoil piles, bars, and deadheads are marked. I'll point them out when I see them. When you see markers with red and green, stay between them. Do not go between two red or two green markers."

"Got it!" I yelled.

We passed the gray Park Service buildings, and Brad slowed the boat to idle. "Beyond here is the part of Padre Island you can't see from the beach. Like the fishermen up ahead, boats don't travel down the channel very far because the water is shallow, and the fishing isn't worth the gas you burn to go farther. Once we get two or three miles past the Park Service buildings, you'll usually be alone. There's a marine-band radio here, by the wheel. It's set on hailing channel sixteen. If you contact someone, plan to meet them on another channel before starting a conversation. If you're in a bind and need backup, Lord help you unless there happens to be a Coast Guard helicopter nearby. There's an outside chance you might be able to contact some agency; the sheriff's department, the city, the division of game and fish, or one of my people, but I wouldn't bet my life on any of them being closer than an hour, or more, away."

I glanced at Matt, who was shaking his head. "Don't stick your neck out. I'd rather have the illegal dumpers get away than have you injured or dead."

I smiled, appreciating his concern for my safety. "There are old cops, and there are bold cops. But there aren't very many old and bold cops."

He nodded and added. "Remember, there's a week of paperwork if you discharge a firearm."

Brad nodded. "It's the same with FWS. If you shoot, you're going to have writer's cramp."

We idled past the two fishing boats to minimize our wake. There were two people in each boat, and they waved as we passed. We waved back, and Brad opened the throttle again once we weren't going to swamp them.

"How do I know where I am if I try to hail someone for help?"

Brad motioned me over to the console and pointed to a display. "Here's a GPS, and it shows your position in latitude and longitude."

"How far are we going? When we drove to the end of the island, we were just past mile marker fifty."

"The fish kill was about a mile ahead. We're not halfway to Port Mansfield channel."

I looked at the GPS. "This isn't very far from the Corpus Christi Bay. I'd expect people doing illegal dumping would go farther from civilization."

Brad shook his head. "As long as they're out of sight of the Park Service buildings and fishermen, why waste gas and time going any farther?"

He throttled back the motor a few minutes later and shifted into neutral, letting the momentum carry the boat ahead slowly. "This is about where we had the report of the dead fish."

Matt looked around to find a landmark. "This looks remarkably like everything else we've passed. And, I don't see any dead fish."

I pointed at some brown bushes on the shoreline. "Can you beach the boat there?"

I heard the whir as the motor tilted. Brad put the motor back in gear. We eased toward the shore until we were about fifteen feet away, then Brad shifted into neutral and shut off the motor, letting our momentum carry us ahead until we heard the hull scraping gently on the bottom. I jumped over the gunwale and felt myself sinking into the mucky bottom. I pulled the boat ahead, struggling to keep my shoes on while the mud sucked at them every time I lifted a foot.

Brad tossed me a line. "Tie us off to a bush."

The shore was slightly less mucky but softer than surf-packed sand on the gulf side of the island. We slogged through swampy muck about twenty yards without seeing anything of interest. I'd gone very slowly, making sure I didn't surprise a rattlesnake.

I stopped to rest. "I doubt anyone dumping pails would bother to walk in this muck to dump their pails. Let's spread out on the walk back."

Matt scanned the scrubby area around us. "What are we looking for?"

Brad was focused on our backtrail. "I suspect we'll find a pile of pails or some ground that looks recently disturbed."

We split up, so we were barely within sight of each other. "Over here!" Brad yelled when we were nearly to the boat.

I took a slightly different path through the bushes. A sickly-sweet chemical smell led me to a depression half-filled with five-gallon pails.

Brad's path took him to the other side of the pails. "It looks like our dumpers were in too much of a hurry to bother burying their stuff." He sniffed the air. "It smells like lacquer thinner."

"They were in too much of a rush to secure the lids." I knelt down to look at an upside-down pail with its lid ajar.

Matt stood behind me with his hands on his hips, carefully staying away from the pails. "They took enough time to paint over the labels. It looks like they spray painted each pail to obscure the label. That'll make it hard to identify the contents or the origin."

Brad waved us away from the pails. "They got smart after the Coast Guard started pulling pails out of the bay. The 'Coasties' were able to identify the pail's recipients, and they tracked the dumping back to a clean-up company. The restoration guys swore they had paperwork showing the hazardous waste had been incinerated and promised the Coast Guard they'd bring in the paperwork the next day. No one's seen them since."

"I don't suppose they were licensed, insured, and bonded."

Brad shook his head. "None of the above. The restoration company showed up in a pickup with a magnetic logo on the side. They gave the owners a low-ball bid for the restoration. There was so much work to be done, and so few contractors, that people weren't too concerned about licenses and insurance. There were a lot of trucks here with license plates from all across the south. Every motel and campground are still filled with workers. Walmart, Kmart, and other Corpus Christi retailers were letting them park RVs in the back of their parking lots. There were a lot of day laborers who lined up at the corner of the highway, and the contractors would come by and choose a few guys, paying them cash each day. It was, and still is, a zoo, and easy pickings for shysters."

I pondered Brad's comments as I untied the line securing the boat to a bush. "So Matt, what are we going to do about this site?"

"I'll start with the Park Service headquarters. I hope they'll direct me to someone who can clean it up. The questions are who, when, and at what cost? There's nothing in the budget for hazardous waste cleanup."

Brad held the boat for Matt. "In the meantime, don't touch anything. If it's killing the bushes and fish, you don't want any of it on your skin, and I think we should move along before we breathe any more fumes. They're probably carcinogenic, if not acutely toxic."

I thought about the chemical-laden muck I'd slogged through and decided to shower and throw away my shoes as soon as I got home. I pushed the boat back and hopped over the gunwale when it started floating. Brad let us drift away from shore before he started the engine and let it idle in reverse until the water was deep enough to lower the motor.

I looked around, making mental notes of the landmarks around us. "Do we think they'll be back?"

Brad put the motor in gear. "Well, there's still rebuilding going on, and they think they got away with dumping around here at least once."

As we eased away from the shore, I thought aloud, "They had to load the pails into the boat somewhere. I assume they didn't do that in daylight at any of the boat launches."

"All they need is a pickup truck, a boat, and a tarp. They could've loaded up their boat anywhere, covered it with a tarp, and launched it somewhere when it wasn't busy."

Chapter 7

I left my shoes and socks on the steps and showered at the townhouse. I dressed in casual clothes. Jill was gone, probably still golfing with the ladies, so I ate cold leftover shrimp with a slice of buttered French bread. I dropped my contaminated socks and tennis shoes in the townhouse dumpster on the way to the pickup.

I sat in my appropriated Park Service office, contemplating people dumping waste. Whatever the pails contained, it was nasty, and my mind ran through the worst-case scenarios of toxic waste, radioactive waste, and biohazards. Any of those items would be bad and require a costly specialized cleanup team. I pondered Brad's comments about a sheen on the water and the fish kill. It had to be some kind of oily chemical waste. I pulled out the Port Aransas yellow pages and flipped through the listings. The businesses selling or using toxic chemicals before the hurricane were too many to list: Boat supplies. Car repair. Gas stations. Pest Control. Hardware stores. Roofing.

The hurricane washed toxic chemicals into the bay and the gulf. Now there were probably over a hundred contractors cleaning up chemicals and doing repairs in the area, each bringing in fresh paint and cleaning chemicals. I searched for government environmental listings on my smartphone and found the Texas Commission on Environmental Quality. I punched in their information number.

After three transfers, I spoke with Sam Gardner, who was polite, diplomatic, and concise. "Pails of toxic waste on Federal property are not the problem of the TCEQ. Since the pails are on Federal property, why don't you contact the EPA?"

It took more transfers at the EPA office in Dallas before connecting to the expert in toxic waste cleanup.

Cheryl Jones sounded cheerful and upbeat, a change from many Federal bureaucrats I'd dealt with through the years. I assumed she wasn't old enough to have become cynical from years of bumping against the Federal bureaucracy. "Ranger Fletcher, how can I be of assistance to the National Park Service?"

"We have an environmental problem. Someone dumped pails of what appears to be toxic waste on the Padre Island National Seashore. We've had a fish kill on Laguna Madre Sound, and the bushes around the dumpsite are dead."

"Do you know who dumped the waste?"

"No. The site is only accessible by boat, and the labels on the pails have been painted over. I suspect the pails were dumped by a contractor doing hurricane cleanup."

"You don't know what the material is, you don't know where it came from, you don't know who dumped it, and you don't know how to clean it up. Does that cover your situation?"

"Aside from not having money for a cleanup, you've nailed my situation exactly."

"This isn't my first rodeo, Fletcher. I get calls with this type of situation at least once a week. I got these calls daily in the months right after the hurricane."

"Will the EPA help me take care of this?"

"I assume you're talking about a dump site smaller than an acre and not filled with drums of waste and cubic yards of contaminated soil. If that's the case, it doesn't fit the threshold of a superfund cleanup site. If so, the EPA won't step in to do the cleanup. I can *suggest* a company who specializes in environmental remediation." I heard computer keys clicking. "I can't *recommend* anyone, but I know Bayliss Environmental works out of Corpus Christi. Their specialty is hazardous material cleanup, and they are licensed, bonded, and insured. They have passed several audits, employ trained technicians, use state of the art cleanup techniques, dispose of recovered materials according to federal and state standards, and their recordkeeping has passed several inspections." She paused. "Have I used enough weasel words to make it sound like they're reputable, but made it clear to you, if they screw up, it's not my problem?"

"I think you covered yourself pretty well. I'll give them a call. Are you willing to assist me in finding the people who dumped the pails?"

"Our investigators are looking at much bigger issues than the illegal disposal of a few pails. If you find out who made the dump, let me know, and I'll send them a threatening 'cease and desist' letter, but I sincerely doubt our lawyers would be willing to chase someone who has dumped less than a thousand gallons of waste. You might have better luck charging them with littering in a National Park."

"I appreciate the feedback, even if it's not what I wanted to hear."

"Believe me, Fletcher, you're not the first person who's said those words to me and, you've put that more politely than about ninety-nine percent of the people I speak with. Thank you."

"You're thanking me?"

"You haven't sworn at me, threatened me, asked to speak with my boss, or torn me a new one. Overall, I'd say you've been quite a gentleman." Jones actually laughed.

"Your job sounds worse than Park Service rangers ticketing speeders. The ticket recipients are unhappy, but rarely make threats."

"I'm not supposed to offer this, but because you've been a gentleman, I'll throw you a bone. FEMA may have hurricane recovery funds to help with your cleanup. When you call them, please don't 'out' me as the person who suggested contacting them."

* * *

I walked into Matt's office and sat in his guest chair as he finished a call.

"What's up?"

"Bayliss Environmental, out of Corpus Christi, does environmental cleanup. A little birdie also told me FEMA may have funds available for hazardous waste removal if you frame the request, so it's part of the hurricane cleanup." I handed him a Post-it note with the Bayliss name and phone number.

"How did you get that information? I've been calling all over the Park Service, and I haven't been able to find a single person who could tell me how to arrange for the cleanup, or who could suggest a way to pay for it except from my operating budget."

"In police jargon, I'd say I have a confidential informant. In military jargon, it'd be from a usually reliable but unidentifiable source."

"Have you spoken with either Bayliss or FEMA?" Matt asked as he scribbled notes.

"I thought I was doing well to come up with options for you."

"Well, yes, you have. I was just hopeful that monkey hadn't jumped on my back."

I got up from his guest chair and smiled. "You're overly optimistic. I imagine Rachel is looking for me. It's time for our afternoon drive down the island."

Matt motioned for me to close his office door. "I'm pleased that you and Rachel are meshing. I was afraid she'd be defensive about having a middle-aged male training officer. When I called her this morning to let her know you and I were going to be away, she sounded disappointed. That's a big endorsement for you."

"I think she might just be relieved to have another person carrying a weapon along on the drive. Or, maybe I'm just someone different to talk to."

"No, she said clearly that she liked having you in the truck with her."

"Well, it's a miserably boring drive, and she's been making it twice a day for a while. I'm sure she's happy to have someone new to talk with. I have some different stories for her."

"There you go, selling yourself short again. It's just like your file says; you do whatever you can to hide from the spotlight and downplay your role in accomplishments. You're a good cop and a good role model for her. I'm even more convinced of that after spending the morning with you."

"I'm just earning my pay." I got up and opened the door. "I'll go find Rachel."

Rachel was leaning on the counter in the visitor center, talking with another female ranger. She waved me over when she saw me. "Doug, this is Melissa Swindell. Missy and I are the lone full-time female rangers stationed here."

I shook Missy's hand. "Nice to meet you.

Missy was blonde except for darker roots, chunky and had acne scars on an otherwise pretty face. Her smile was genuine, and she seemed to be surprised when I offered to shake hands with her.

"Hi, Doug." She had a distinctive Texas twang. "Nice to meet you. Rachel says you're a pretty nice guy, for a Yankee."

"For a Yankee? You had to qualify the nice guy comment with that, Rachel?"

"I didn't call you a Yankee." Rachel held up her hands defensively. "I just said you were from Minnesota. Missy is responsible for interpreting the geography."

"Shush, you two." Missy pointed toward a family that had just walked in. "Y'all get out of here before you scare them away with your guns."

"I thought everyone down here carried a gun," I said, smiling.

"We do, but I don't want them to think the rangers are carrying too."

Rachel and I walked to the Park Service pickup. "Missy seems nice."

"She is, but you'd best be careful. She just broke up with a guy who worked on an offshore drilling platform, and she's trolling for a new boyfriend. Did you notice her checking your finger for a wedding ring?"

balloons on the sand. Each one's got a little pocket of air that pops when the tires roll over them."

I looked down the beach ahead of the truck. There are thousands of them. "I suppose children find them irresistible. They probably run down the beach popping them."

"Yup, and every second little kid who sees one thinks he has to pick it up and gets stung by the tentacles."

"What's the first aid for a sting?"

"Well, the folk remedy is peeing on it. Obviously, that treatment is more easily applied by guys than women." Rachel checked for my reaction. I failed to smile, so she went on, "The modern treatment is to spray vinegar solution on the sting. I don't know that the vinegar actually does anything, but it seems to have a placebo effect if nothing else."

"We used MSG on bee stings when I was in Scouts."

"I've heard that works, too, but we don't keep any meat tenderizer in the first aid kit." Without missing a beat, Rachel added, "You changed the topic. What's your relationship status?"

"That sounds like a Facebook question."

"You're being evasive."

"Yes, I am."

"It's going to be a long drive if I have to keep hounding you."

"Jill Rickowski was my Flagstaff boss. S¹ was interested in my investigations, and e evening I'd call her with an update. After the first investigation was over, I went to Federal law enforcement training in Georgia. The night I left for training she told me I felt like her peer, and my calls were the first comfortable conversations she'd had with a co-worker in years. She said she was going to miss them."

"You walked away after a lead-in like that?"

"Not entirely. Jill called me a couple times to see how training was going, then I called her a couple times when the nights felt empty. I graduated and was ready to move here. Then she called, asking me to come back to Flagstaff because she had a mystery requiring an investigator. We got back into the cycle of evening calls, then we wound up together on a backcountry trip. We spent a couple days talking as we hiked. Her job got complicated, she was put on leave during an investigation, and I asked if she'd like to come along to Texas until her job situation got sorted out. She said, 'okay.'"

"You glossed over something."

"What?"

"She invited you over for a drink, and you spent the night." Rachel glanced at me when I didn't respond. "That was it, wasn't it?"

"We went out for supper and discovered we'd become best friends. Neither of us was ready to walk away from that."

"Your place or hers?"

"What makes you think . . ."

"You're so old-fashioned."

"What's old-fashioned about that?"

Rachel kept her focus on the beach. "Now, the sparks fly, and we find out if the physical part of the relationship works. If it does, we hang out together until we become besties. Or, we start fighting and move on."

"If you're 'besties' and the physical part is working, do you get married?"

"That's kind of old-fashioned. If you're popping out kidlets, then you probably get married. But if your relationship is just cruising along comfortably, why complicate things with a marriage license? I mean, things can still go to crap, and a marriage license means you go through a divorce. If you're not married and things fall apart, one of you packs up and moves away. It's so much easier."

"You have to work at making a marriage work," I said.

"How did that work out for you? You said you're divorced. Did your ex move on and start sleeping with one of her college buddies? Did you work at making that work, or did you just let her go and feel relieved?"

"Relieved. Life had been stressful, and part of that was because I was a cop. It's tough being married to a cop."

"You're taking responsibility for something you didn't cause. It's not like you pushed her into some guy's arms. She went willingly." When I didn't immediately respond, Rachel asked, "So, what's going on with you and your roomie? You said you were best friends. She moved to Texas with you. I assume you're sharing a bed. Does that mean there's an old-fashioned wedding on the horizon?"

"Not yet."

"Still feeling the burn of the divorce?"

"There's some of that, but we have careers that might be going in different directions. I get the impression the Park Service isn't particularly concerned about moving couples to places where both of them are needed."

"Most rangers that I know are single or divorced. The married ones usually have made a career commitment to the Park Service, and their spouse trails along when they get a new posting." Rachel looked surprised. "Hey, we're already to Shell Beach."

"Great! Let's take a break and stretch our legs."

"There's a tent ahead of us. We can talk to the campers, too."

A young woman, wearing a bikini top and cut-off denim shorts dashed out of the dunes and raced to the surf. She squatted down and put something into the water from her cupped hands.

"What's she up to?" I asked as I unbuckled my seatbelt.

"I think she's found baby sea turtles." The pickup rolled to a stop.

The skinny and athletic girl looked like she might've been in her teens. She waved at us and dashed back into the dunes. We stood in front of the pickup and watched. A moment later, a young man with a scraggly beard and long hair and slightly older than the girl, dashed from the dunes with something cupped in his hands. He seemed surprised to see us, but it didn't slow down his dash toward the surf.

"I got two of them!" he yelled as he passed. Seagulls swarmed over his head as he waded into the surf until he was up to his ribs, then he released his catch, waving his arms to keep the seagulls away.

"The seagulls think of baby turtles as appetizers," Rachel explained. "Most often the hatchlings come out in the dark when there are fewer predators around. If they come out in the daylight, and if there's no one like these two to help, hardly any of the hatchlings ever make it to the water before something eats them."

"I think this is the last one!" the girl yelled as she raced past. Her sun-bleached blonde hair waved in the wind as she waded into the water.

We watched the girl carry the sea turtle hatchling to where the surf was breaking and set it gently into the waves. She watched for a few seconds, then waded back to us. Her boyfriend had already joined us next to the pickup. I relaxed. After years as a cynical cop, I was prepared for every encounter with a civilian to turn into a confrontation, but this guy's casual-friendly approach put me at ease.

"You guys weren't here this morning when I drove by," Rachel said to the guy as we watched the blonde girl slog her way through the surf.

"We came through the gate about noon and drove down after we picnicked near your buildings. It's okay for us to camp here, isn't it?"

"You're fine as long as you don't dump anything or litter. Lots of people camp on the beach."

The guy eyed me suspiciously. I was out of uniform, and my shirt did little to hide the bulge of the pistol on my hip. I'd forgotten to pin on my badge when I changed at the townhouse.

The girl bounded up the shore to us, beaming like she'd just saved the planet. "I feel really good about saving the baby turtles."

Rachel smiled. "They don't stand much of a chance against the gulls. I doubt any of them would've made it to the surf without your intervention."

I guessed we were nearly opposite the area where we'd found the pails on the other side of the island, so I decided to mine them for information. "We've been having some issues with people coming up the backside of the island in boats. Have you heard any motors since you got here?"

The girl shrugged and looked at the guy. "We haven't heard anything."

The guy continued to eye my pistol suspiciously, which made my skin prickly. "Do you have something illegal in the tent?" The girl gave the guy a fearful look, making me even more suspicious.

I walked to the tent and peeked through the open flap. They'd thrown a couple of backpacks and blankets into the nylon tent. The interior was lit with a glow by the sun passing through the orange nylon. I was about to stand up when I noticed a plastic bag containing a joint sticking out of the side pocket of a backpack.

The guy walked over and squatted next to me. "Are you some kind of cop?"

"I'm a Park Service investigator."

"Why are you snooping around? We just came to camp and get away."

I noted the Kansas license plates on the Jeep as I stood. "I've got no beef with you. What do you guys do back in Kansas?"

"I work for a landscaping business. Cait is a waitress."

"If I run your license plate, it's not going to come back with any outstanding warrants, is it?"

"We're clean." He was either a good liar, or he was being honest.

"How about you, Cait?" I asked the girl. "Do you have any outstanding warrants? No one's reported you missing?"

Cait's eyes darted to the guy, waiting for him to reply. "She's clean, too."

"Cait, can you answer the question yourself?"

"Sure. There aren't any warrants for me."

I looked at her skeptically. "Is someone looking for you?"

Rachel stepped away from the truck and stood alongside Cait, putting a hand on her shoulder. "Are you okay?"

The guy took a step toward the girl, but I got between them. "Let's talk over by your Jeep." I directed him away from Rachel and Cait. Between the burbling surf and the squawking gulls, we couldn't hear what Rachel and Cait said, but the girl was very animated.

"What's your name?"

"I don't have to give you my name. You said you're an investigator and obviously carrying a gun, but that doesn't give you any right to question me."

I reached for my wallet, and the guy winced. "Easy. I'm getting my I.D." I showed him my badge and credentials. "See, I'm a Federal investigator."

The guy glanced at the badge, then gave me a sour look. "Cait's mom might be looking for her— if she's sobered up."

"If Cait's an adult, that's not a problem. If she's under eighteen, she's considered a runaway." If he was having sex with her, he could be in deep trouble both in state and federal courts.

"Her mother's boyfriend visited Cait's bedroom and raped her. She asked me to take her away."

"Did she tell her mother about the abuse?"

The guy let out a sigh. "Her mom didn't believe her and told Cait if anything happened it was because of the skimpy outfits she wore around the house."

"Do you want to tell me about the marijuana I saw in your backpack?"

The guy shook his head. "That's private property. You can't search without a warrant."

"Anything in plain sight is fair game. You left the tent flap open and made it the same as looking in through the window of a car. Because you're on the National Seashore, drug possession and use are Federal crimes, not the misdemeanors you'd be facing if you were off the Park Service land. Do you understand?"

"Yeah."

"What's your name?"

"Paul Argento."

"How old are you, Paul?"

"Eighteen."

"What's Cait's last name, and how old is she?"

"Her name is Caitlyn Robinson. She told me she's eighteen."

"She told you she's eighteen. Does she have a driver's license, Paul?"

"She forgot it when we left."

"Any chance she isn't old enough to drive?"

"Listen, man, Cait's really messed up, and I'm trying to get her out of a bad situation. She's here because she asked me to take her away. I'm trying to do the right thing."

"Do you have any weapons on yourself, in the tent, or in the car?"

"There's a hunting knife in the back of the Jeep, in the cooler with our food. We don't have any guns if that's what you're asking."

"How about needles, razor blades, or drugs?"

"We smoked the one joint on the way down. The one you saw is the last. Okay?"

"Are you willing to sit quietly by the Jeep, or do I need to cuff you while I talk with Caitlyn and my partner?"

"What am I going to do, run back to the highway?" The guy sat in the sand and leaned his elbows on his knees. I walked to Rachel and Caitlyn. The girl was crying and wiped her nose on her wrist.

"Things are pretty bad at home?" I asked.

Caitlyn nodded, and Rachel looked shocked. "What did he say to you?" Rachel asked. I signaled her to wait.

"Paul told me what was going on. I'd like to hear your side before I decide what to do."

Cait's eyes shot to Paul, who shrugged. "We had to get away from Emporia. My stepdad was all over me every time we were alone. I asked Paul to take me someplace safe."

I softened my voice, realizing the trauma she'd faced, and not wanting to add to it. "How old are you, Cait?"

"Seventeen."

"You told Paul you were eighteen, but you don't have a driver's license. Are you fifteen?"

Cait looked stricken. "I had to get out of there."

"Paul could be in deep trouble for taking you across the Kansas state line," I watched her eyes. "Are you two being intimate?"

"It's not like he's *making* me do anything." Cait broke into tears. "And it's not like we're doing anything my stepfather hasn't already forced me to do."

Rachel put her hand on Cait's arm. "It's okay. You're safe now."

Cait looked at me, her eyes pleading. "What about Paul? He's been helping me, and I don't want to get him into trouble."

Paul had been staring at the ground. He looked at me, waiting to see what I was going to do. "We're not arresting anyone, but we have to contact the police in your hometown. I'll ask Paul to pack up the tent and follow us back to the visitor center where we can make some calls."

"No! I can't go back. My mom doesn't believe me."

"Do you have a different safe place to stay?" Rachel asked.

"Yeah. I've got an aunt in Kansas City. I can call her and maybe stay there."

I walked Paul to the tent. He asked, "How deep is the shit?"

"Cait's going to call her aunt in Kansas City, and I'll have to call the Emporia Police. I think we can sort this all out."

"I was trying to be a nice guy, and I'm going to be in trouble."

"I respect what you were trying to do." I helped him break down the tent. "Follow us back to the visitor center. We'll make some calls and get things sorted out."

"You're not going to arrest me?"

"Cait says you rescued her. I don't usually arrest people who are in the rescue business."

"Are you really a cop?"

"Just because I'm a cop doesn't mean I have to be a jerk. Now, if we get back, and I find out you kidnapped Cait, or you've got outstanding warrants and an arrest record as long as my arm, I might feel differently. But that's not the vibe I'm getting off you."

"Thanks."

"Follow us back to the visitor center and lose the joint before you come inside."

Rachel drove the pickup with Caitlyn in the front. I sat in the back and listened to their dialogue.

"I don't want to go back to Mom. It was…"

"What else was going on in your life?"

"I played clarinet in the band and was a midfielder on the soccer team. Mom used to come to my concerts and games. We were a family and did family things. Then Jack showed up, and suddenly, I was invisible. I'd come home from school and do my homework, just like I always had, but I was never sure if Mom was going to be there at suppertime. I'd make myself something out of a can or the freezer and watch tv or talk to people on the phone. I'd go to bed, then I'd hear them laughing downstairs.

They drank every night. They'd go to bed, and then sometimes, I'd hear someone walking in the hallway. Jack would climb in bed with me after Mom went to sleep." Cait started to cry.

"We'll get you some help, but we need to let your mom know you're safe."

Cait sniffled back her tears. "She doesn't care where I am. She and Jack made me get a job working as a waitress, so they could pay the bills because they drank so much Mom got fired. I was having a hard time with school because I had to go to the restaurant for the supper rush. Then I'd have to hang around until all the dishwashers were done before the boss would split up the tips. It was usually so late I was too tired to do homework, so I got behind in my classes. Paul would come into the house some nights after driving me home. He'd hang around to make sure Jack wasn't visiting my bedroom." Cait stopped abruptly.

"There was something else, wasn't there?"

"Jack came home with a bunch of guys to play poker one night. He was losing, and apparently, he told the guys they could go up to my bedroom if he lost..." Cait started sobbing. "I called Paul the next morning, and we left."

Rachel glanced at me in the rear-view mirror. I took out my phone and found the website for Texas Child Protective Services (CPS), a division of the Texas Department of Family Protective Services (DFPS). I dialed the abuse hotline and quietly spoke with the person who answered the 24-hour hotline while Rachel and Cait talked.

"This is Douglas Fletcher, from the National Park Service. We have a Kansas teen runaway who's been abused by her stepfather. I'm stationed at the Padre Island National Seashore, off Corpus Christi. How do I get this girl to a safe place?"

"Mr. Fletcher, are you a Park Service ranger?"

"I'm an investigator for the NPS. We found this young woman and her boyfriend camping. She's fifteen, and she's running away from a situation where her stepfather had been abusing her and pimping her out to his friends. I don't have the resources through the Park Service to deal with her needs."

"Has her mother reported her missing?"

"I don't know. We just picked her up at a campsite, and we're taking her to our headquarters building. Can you get someone to pick her up, assess her situation, and get her to a safe place?"

"Is she with you now?" the woman on the hotline asked.

"Yes. We're in a Park Service vehicle, and she's riding in the front seat with my partner."

"Hang on while I pull up the database of missing and exploited children." I heard keys clicking. "Give me her name, please."

"Caitlyn Robinson. She's from Emporia, Kansas," I said.

"Got it," the woman said. "She's listed as a possible abductee from Emporia. Can you hand her the phone and let me talk to her?"

"Cait, I have someone on the phone who can help you. Will you talk to her?"

Cait took the phone. I caught snippets of conversation over the singing of the tires on the sand. I checked behind us, and Paul's black Jeep followed in our tracks. Cait started crying as she talked on the phone. Rachel kept looking at me in the mirror like I was supposed to have the answer to Caitlyn's situation.

Cait handed the phone back over the seat. "They're going to have someone meet us at the Park Service headquarters," she said. "They have to call Mom, but they promised they wouldn't make me go back home. But Paul can't come with me. They said…" she started to cry.

I knew no child protection agency would allow an underage teen to stay with her adult boyfriend. "They won't let you stay with him because you're too young."

Cait nodded.

"If they have a safe place for you to stay, is that okay?"

I looked at her profile and realized she could've been my child. She should've been having a fun life filled with school, sports, and band. Instead, she was running away from an abusive pimp who was using her mother to get to Cait.

"Rachel, take Caitlyn to Matt's office while we get a plan together." I waited in the parking lot for the Jeep. Paul parked alongside the NPS pickup.

"Where's Cait?" he asked.

"She's going to the park superintendent's office. I spoke with Texas Child Protective Services. They've got someone coming to take Cait to a safe place until they can sort out a plan. Cait suggested going to her Aunt's house in Kansas City."

Paul looked numb. He nodded. "I guess I'm not in the picture."

"Because Caitlyn's only fifteen, I'm afraid she has to be treated as a missing minor child, and you can't be with her. It's in your best interest to disappear. When Child Protection Services finds out you helped her escape, there will be questions. Because you're an adult who took an underaged child across state lines, you could face both state and federal charges. That'll be complicated by the fact you've been intimate with her."

Paul nodded. "So, I should trust you'll find Cait a safe place that doesn't involve her going back to Jack and her mom."

"Let's go inside." I steered him toward the Park Service buildings. "I'll buy you a can of pop and a bag of chips."

I left Paul in the Park Service break room while I called the Corpus Christi Police. I was connected with David Palmer, a desk sergeant. After identifying myself, he looked up Paul's criminal record on the National Crime Information Computer (NCIC).

"He's got a couple speeding tickets he paid up, but no wants or warrants," Palmer said. "Did you arrest him for abducting the girl?"

"She's a runaway, not a kidnap victim. I've got CPS coming to pick her up. He's been taking care of her, so I don't want to arrest him for his role in her escape."

I could hear the computer keys clicking. "Emporia has a 'find and hold' order out for Caitlyn Robinson. They list her as a possible stranger abduction. If you've got the guy who abducted her, they'll want you to hold him pending kidnapping charges. Is he in your custody?"

"The last I saw of him, he was in our parking lot," I said.

"Give me his license number and a description of his vehicle, and we'll watch for him. If we can't catch him before he gets out of Corpus Christi, I'm sure the rangers can find him before he gets out of Texas."

I had visions of Paul being held in some small-town jail until Emporia sent someone down to pick him up, or until they decided they weren't interested in prosecuting him. "No, I'll take him into custody here and contact Emporia. Thanks."

Paul sat in the break room, staring at the coffee pot. He flinched when he heard me walk in. "What's up?" he asked.

"I'm going to hold you until I can talk with the Emporia police. I think I can convince them to drop their order to find and hold you on kidnapping charges."

"Kidnapping?"

"It's complicated because Caitlyn is so young," I sat in the chair across the table. "I understand you're trying to save her from an abusive situation, but her mother reported her missing and possibly kidnapped. That really complicates your situation."

"So, you're going to arrest me?"

"Child Protective Services is going to pick Caitlyn up and take her away, maybe to a hospital for an exam and treatment. Then she'll probably go to a shelter for abused women. They'll contact her mother, but if Cait tells them the same story we heard, I suspect the Emporia police will be questioning her stepfather and mother, and they may press charges against them."

"But where does that leave me?"

"Do you have money for gas?"

"I've got a credit card."

"Fill up your tank and head somewhere other than Kansas."

"What?"

"Get out of here. Drive somewhere."

"But I don't know where to go."

"Let me tell you what's going on." I gave him my best cop voice. "Once Cait starts talking to CPS, your name is going to come up. Until then, Emporia doesn't know who you are, and you're still a free man. Go west, to maybe Phoenix or Albuquerque. Find a job as a day laborer and let things cool off in Kansas."

"What's the alternative, like if I want to hang around until Cait gets free?"

"First of all, Cait's not *getting free*. She's not eighteen, and that means she's going back to Kansas and if not with her mother, to her aunt, or into a foster home. Secondly, I'll have to arrest you, and Corpus Christi police will hold you in jail until Emporia decides if they want to pick you up. I think they'll decide they don't want to spend the money, but it might take them a couple weeks for some prosecutor to work his way through his pile of cases and make a decision about charging you with kidnapping. All the while, you'll sit in a Texas jail cell with a bunch of drunks and criminals. If Emporia gets a district attorney with a bug up his behind, he might contact the Feds about charging you for taking Cait out of state for sexual purposes, which is a big-time Federal offense—the Mann Act. Again, I doubt the Feds will want to charge you once they understand the circumstances, but they may keep you locked up for a few days, while they question you, Cait, and her mother about her disappearance. If you get a tough Federal prosecutor, he or she might decide to prosecute, and you could end up in Federal prison for a long time."

Paul stared at his hands, clasped in his lap.

"Like I said, I'm giving you the gift of freedom. Get out of here and stay away from

Kansas for a while. I'd go west. There are jobs, and you're a long way from the reach of Emporia. Don't break the speed limit and get rid of the joint if it's still sticking out of your backpack."

I stood up and waited a second for Paul to make up his mind. He finally stood but looked dazed.

"Can I camp here for a couple days to see what happens?"

"Somebody is going to call me and ask where you are. I need deniability. I have to be able to say you left, and I don't know where you've gone." I put out my hand, and we shook.

"Thank you."

"You're welcome, and I hope this works. And if you get picked up somewhere, we never had this discussion."

He looked at my shirt to see if I was wearing a name tag. "I don't know your name."

"It's better for both of us if you don't remember who I am."

"What about Cait's stuff?" he asked.

"I'll give it to her."

We walked to the Jeep, and he handed me Cait's pink backpack. "That's all she brought."

I watched him dig through the back of his Jeep, then he threw something, I hoped the joint, into a garbage container. After he pulled out of the lot, I walked to Matt's office. Cait was still in tears. I pulled a chair out of the break room and brought it into the office and closed the door. I set her backpack next to the desk.

"Where's Paul?" Cait asked.

"He had to leave."

"Without me?" she wailed.

"I'm sorry, Cait, but your situation is out of our control. When I spoke with Texas Child Protective Services, they said you're listed on the national database of missing and exploited children as possibly kidnapped. Any agency who finds you is legally obligated to hold you, notify your local police, and to arrest the person you're with. CPS is sending someone who will make sure you have a safe place to stay. We have to notify the Emporia Police Department we've found you."

"But, Paul?"

"Paul could be in big trouble because you're listed as a kidnapping."

"I want to see him."

"He's gone."

Cait wailed, and Rachel dabbed at her own eyes with a tissue from a box on Matt's desk.

"Matt, can you find a non-emergency phone number for the Emporia police?" I asked.

Matt punched a few computer keystrokes and then picked up his landline. He dialed the number, then held out the phone. "Do you want to talk to them?"

I took the phone as it was answered in Kansas. "This is Douglas Fletcher, an investigator with the National Park Service, stationed in Texas. We are sitting in an office with a young woman who's listed as a possible kidnap victim. Her name is Caitlyn Robinson."

"Hang on, Fletcher. I'll connect you with one of our detectives."

I activated the speakerphone, and we listened to elevator music for nearly a minute.

"What are they going to do?" Cait asked.

"This is Detective Smith. Am I speaking with Ranger Fletcher?"

"This is Fletcher. I'm in the park superintendent's office at the Padre Island National Seashore. I've got you on speakerphone with Park Superintendent Matt Mattson, Ranger Rachel Randall, and Caitlyn Robinson. We located Caitlyn this afternoon and discovered you've been looking for her."

"Wow! She's only been gone for three days, and she made it all the way to Texas. Are you there, Caitlyn?"

"Yup."

"Your mom's been worried about you," Smith said. His voice was reassuring.

"I doubt that. My mom let my stepfather rape me, and when I told her, she said it was a lie and if it wasn't a lie, it was because I was running around the house in skimpy clothes."

The phone went silent.

"Are you still there, detective?" I asked.

"Yeah. Sorry. I was making some notes. That's quite an accusation, Caitlyn."

"My friends call me Cait."

"Okay, Cait. I'd like to make arrangements to get you back here."

"I'm not going back to live in a house with the man who raped me."

"Um, certainly not. Um, we'll have to talk to some folks here about what we can do to accommodate you while I look into your accusations. Fletcher, are you still there?"

"Yes, detective."

"Can you put Caitlyn, I mean Cait, into some sort of a protected place while I make arrangements on my end?"

"I've contacted Texas Child Protective Services, and they've got someone coming to pick her up. By the way, I've spoken with Cait at some length, and I believe her claims about her stepfather."

"Yeah, well, that's going to take some interviews and work on our end. I think it's pretty clear we can't let Cait go back to her mama if her stepfather is still living there."

"This is Matt Mattson, the park superintendent. Thank you for reassuring us. We've taken a liking to Cait, and we're concerned about her wellbeing. If there is anyone in a child protection group I can contact, please let me know, and I'll be happy to lean on them to do what's best for Cait. I assume some pressure from a Federal agency might break loose some resources."

"Thanks for your concern, superintendent. I think we're pretty well equipped to take care of Cait. I'll make a call to the county as soon as we're off the phone, and then I'll call Cait's mama to let her know she's safe. On second thought, I think I'll drive over and tell her. That way, I can have a discussion with her stepfather.

Cait, is there anyone who you've told about your stepfather? Maybe a friend who could corroborate your story?"

I put my finger to my lips and shook my head. "Not Paul," I whispered in her ear.

"I haven't really told any of my friends. I didn't think…I was embarrassed. I mean, you don't tell people a guy is sneaking into your bedroom when your mother is passed out."

"I don't suppose you've got a hidden camera in the room or something that could serve as evidence of his actions."

"No camera. Sorry, there's just my word." Cait started to sob.

I had a thought. "Cait, is there any clothing lying around that you might've worn after he assaulted you?"

"I imagine my nightgown in under my pillow. It's not like Mom would've done any of my laundry. Wait! And there are underpants I wore. They're probably still on the bedroom floor."

"Atta girl," Smith said. "You've given me something to work with. Fletcher, can you give me the phone number for Texas CPS? I'll contact them and confirm their plans for Cait's care until we can get her back."

I motioned for Rachel to pull the information up on her cellphone. "We're going to feed Cait and wait for CPS. She's pretty hungry and tired after hitchhiking all the way down here."

Matt scowled at me and mouthed, "hitchhiked?" I nodded.

"I was wondering how she'd got all the way to Texas. We'd kind of been working off the theory she was hiding out with some friends locally, although we've pretty well gone through everyone she knows at school."

"She said a guy driving a Jeep picked her up outside Emporia, and he was headed for Texas, so she just hung with him."

"Are you okay? He didn't force you into his vehicle, offer you drugs, or take advantage of you, Cait?" Smith asked.

"He was a perfect gentleman."

"Did you get his name?"

"His first name was Paul."

"Okay, then. It looks like I've got my work cut out for me. We're really pleased you're healthy and safe. It sounds like the Park Service is looking out for you, Cait. If there's nothing else, Fletcher, I'll start making some phone calls and work on a search warrant."

I leaned close to the speaker. "There's another complication. Caitlyn said her stepfather had some drunken buddies over for poker, and when he went bust, he sent them up to Cait's room to collect."

"That's quite an accusation."

"Detective Smith, this is Superintendent Mattson, Cait seems credible. I think her story is worth checking out."

"I've noted that, and we'll certainly check it out."

"Thank you, detective. I'm pleased you're taking Cait's story seriously and taking ownership of this case."

"I've got an eleven-year-old daughter, Fletcher. Believe me, I'm going to look after Cait's case as if I were doing it for my own daughter."

"Detective, this is Matt Mattson again. Please call me with an update when Cait gets back to Emporia. We're all invested in her story, and I want to personally make sure she's put in a situation where she can go back to being a kid again."

"I've got your number on my caller ID. I'll get back to you."

Chapter 8

"Honey, I'm home," I called out as I walked into the townhouse.

"Who do you think you are, a character from a 1960s sitcom?" Jill called back from the kitchen. We hugged in the hallway, and she gave me a quick kiss. "Get changed. I've almost got supper ready."

The Texas coastal humidity left me feeling sticky all the time, so I took a quick shower. Jill had tidied the bedroom, and my mostly clean shorts had disappeared from the chair by the bed. I found them clean and folded, in a dresser drawer. I pulled on a Minnesota Twins t-shirt that felt damp in the drawer, and I strapped on a pair of leather sandals that had appeared on my side of the bed.

"You've become very domestic." I sat in a kitchen chair. The table was set with plates, silverware, and tall, frosty glasses of iced tea, each garnished with a lemon wedge.

"I hope you like iced tea." Jill carried a steaming bowl of spaghetti to the table. She went back to the kitchen and returned with a bowl of pasta sauce dotted with meatballs.

"I don't have any negative feelings about iced tea," I said, taking a sip and bracing for the sweetness. "This isn't sweet tea."

"I know it's a Southern tradition, but I don't need the calories in sweet tea." She pulled up her chair and reached for the pasta.

"I'm impressed how you timed the pasta perfectly, considering you didn't know exactly when I'd be home."

"It's a trick I learned as a waitress in college. You parboil the noodles, then dunk them in boiling water to reheat them just before you're ready to serve." She passed the pasta to me.

"How was golf?"

"I was terrible, but Mandy's friends were tolerant and funny. They treated me like an old friend and said I'm welcome to join them any time. Mandy is going to pick me up again next week."

"Matt warned Mandy about Peg Leg Pete's. What was that about?"

Jill laughed. "It looks like a rundown old building with fishnets and junk hanging from the ceiling. The menu was a chalkboard featuring local seafood and beer. I had redfish, and the serving was huge, and the sauce was to die for. Matt's warning was because the women drink Bloody Marys after golf, and they get a little loud."

"Were the Bloody Marys spicy?"

"I tried a sip of Mandy's, and it lit my South Dakota mouth on fire. They had a big jug of peppers marinating in Vodka, and that's what they use in the drinks. I wasn't quite up to drinking after last night, so I stuck with Diet Coke and endured a lot of friendly kidding." Jill paused and asked, "How was fishing?"

"We didn't fish. It was a boat ride through the Laguna Madre on the backside of Padre Island. We found a toxic waste dump site on a Park Service shore this morning. I went slogging through the contaminated muck and threw my shoes away. All my other clothing went right into the washer."

"Is that his boat in our parking lot?"

"Matt's friend works for the Fish and Wildlife Service. He left the boat with me for a few days, so I can continue to check out the backside of Padre Island."

"That explains the boat and trailer parked outside the townhouse. I assume that means you'll be making regular patrols of the Laguna Madre, trying to catch the people dumping waste."

"Since Matt's friend loaned me the boat for a few days, I thought you might like to take a ride tomorrow morning."

"Are you leaving at oh-dark-thirty again?" Her tone made it clear she was not interested in getting up that early.

"We can go whenever you get ready," I discerned the proper response.

Jill smiled. "You are learning."

"You're becoming a domestic goddess."

"What qualifies me as a domestic goddess?"

"The bedroom is immaculate. You took my clothes out of the washer, put them in the dryer, folded them, and put everything away in the right drawers. Your outfit is nicely put together, you're wearing a touch of lipstick, and supper was ready when I walked in the door. You must've spent the whole afternoon cleaning, cooking, and making yourself beautiful."

Jill smiled, and her dimples showed. "Thank you. After lunch, I went to the gym for an hour, cleaned, and started reading a book. By the way, if we go out in the boat, I have to be back by one to play bridge."

"Bridge?"

"One of the women at the gym was looking for a fourth to fill in tomorrow. One of their regulars has to go to CC tomorrow afternoon."

"I didn't know you played bridge?"

"I haven't played in years, but my grandma used to draft me to fill in when she needed a fourth player for her tea group. I learned when I was ten. By the time I went to college, I was pretty good. I imagine that will all come back to me. I haven't played in thirty years." Jill paused and then asked, "Tell me more about what happened during your day?"

"We found a young couple rescuing baby sea turtles and camping on the shore. The guy looked suspicious, so I looked inside their tent and saw a joint sticking out of a backpack. We questioned them and found out the girl was

97

fifteen and had run away from an abusive home situation. We got her connected with Texas Child Protection Services, and then called the police in her hometown."

"What kind of an abusive situation?"

"She said her stepfather visited her bedroom when her mother got drunk and passed out."

"Oh, God." Jill wiped her mouth with a paper napkin. "That's terrible. You're not sending her back to her mother and stepfather, are you?"

"The Kansas detective we spoke to sounded like he had his head on straight. He talked about getting a search warrant for the mother's house and exploring options for getting the girl back to school in a safe environment."

Jill reached out and squeezed my hand. "You weren't tempted to drive to Kansas and shoot the sonofabitch?"

"I got past that twenty years ago. I can't save every child, nor can I apply my own justice to every criminal. I do the best I can, and let the system do the rest."

"I hope they put the stepfather in jail."

"I hope so too. And if he goes to prison, he's going to suffer more than anything I'd ever do to him."

"He'll get a few years in prison. That's not a terrible punishment." Jill returned to her spaghetti.

"Prison populations don't like child molesters. He'll spend his prison years watching his back and having a hard time sleeping."

Jill appeared to weigh my words as she ate, then suddenly pushed her chair back from the table, and I wondered if she was reacting to scenes of the child molester in prison. "The domestic goddess failed." She rushed into the kitchen. The refrigerator opened, and she walked back holding two bowls of salad with cucumber and tomato slices on top. "I forgot the salads."

I got up and kissed her on top of the head. "You also forgot the dressing." I hurried into the kitchen for the two bottles of salad dressing in the refrigerator and set them on the table. She took the Western dressing, and I opened the Italian. "I guess that proves you aren't perfect. What were you reading?"

"I went to the library and found a book by Lori Armstrong. Her protagonist is a female Army sniper who returns to her South Dakota ranch after getting mentally messed up in Iraq. It's really got me hooked."

"I didn't know you were into mysteries."

"I've never been a mystery fan, but I read a review of this book in the paper. The South Dakota setting and the character are so close to home that I'm really getting into it. I feel connected to this single woman who's attempting to get her life back together after her military career turns her upside down."

"I guess I never saw you as a reader."

"I haven't ever read a book for fun in years. I used to enjoy some of the literature class assignments in junior high, but I burned out on the classics in high school. I never had time to read for fun in college or do anything that seemed so self-indulgent when I was working."

"Is walking on the beach after supper self-indulgent?"

Jill smiled. "I'd categorize that as romantic."

"Your dimples make you look like a teenager."

"You are so full of shit."

"That may be true, but your smile says you like me that way."

"Finish your spaghetti so we can get to the beach before dark."

Chapter 9

Laguna Madre Wednesday morning

I let Rachel know I wouldn't be there for the morning beach patrol, then I hooked the boat trailer to the Park Service pickup. Jill watched me from the back steps with a cup of steaming coffee in her hand.

"Are you ready to go for the boat ride?" I asked.

"I thought you were kidding. This is part of an investigation."

"It is. So what?"

"You can't take a civilian along when you're investigating."

"You've still got a Park Service badge and you're collecting a salary, so I think we could legitimately say I've asked you along on temporary duty."

Jill considered that for a moment. "Give me a second to put a lid on my coffee and grab my badge." She returned five minutes later wearing a floppy hat, carrying a beach bag, and smearing sunscreen on her arms.

By eight o'clock, we were slowly boating down the Laguna Madre.

Jill's head swiveled as she took in the surroundings. "I can't believe it's so wild this close to CC."

"What's CC?"

"Oh, the women at the gym always refer to Corpus Christi as CC rather than saying the words every two sentences."

"I think it's wild because the water is shallow and muddy, and the area on the mainland side is swampy and inaccessible by road most of the way to Port Mansfield channel. I was warned to go slow, stay in the middle of the channel, and watch for sandbars and deadheads."

"I'm surprised there were only two other trailers in the parking lot. It seems like this would be a great fishing area."

"Brad Johnson, from the Fish and Wildlife Service, said weekdays are quiet. People from inland come out here on the weekends, and then it gets busy."

I saw a red fishing boat in the distance and angled toward it. There were two men in it, on the front and rear platforms. They had fishing rods in their hands and seemed to be just staring at the water. As we got near, they reeled their lines in and set their rods aside. I killed the motor and drifted up until the man in the rear put his foot out and stopped us from bumping the boat.

"Anything biting?" I asked.

They appraised us curiously. "Not much today." The man in the rear opened the live well and lifted out an eighteen-inch fish. "Just one speckled trout."

Both men were well past retirement age. They wore broad-brimmed hats, long-sleeved shirts, and nylon pants that dried quickly.

The man in the front had gauze covering his left ear. "You don't look like the game warden. He checked our licenses last week, and he doesn't come out with a pretty woman."

That comment got a smile from Jill. "Thank you."

"You ought to be covered up better. The sun out here is brutal, and you young folks don't understand the damage." He touched his ear. "I just lost half my ear to skin cancer. I used to laugh it off when the doctor scolded me for not wearing sunscreen. Now, he told me to cover up, or he'd be lopping off body parts every year until they started chemo. He kinda got my attention this time."

"Thanks for the warning." Jill had stowed her hat while we were motoring. She pulled it out of her beach bag and put it on.

"I work for the Park Service," I explained. "Somebody's been dumping pails of chemicals on the island. Have you seen any boats going through here that didn't look like they were fishing?"

They looked at each other, apparently considering their answer, which made me wonder whether they were going to give me a truthful answer. Finally, the man in front nodded to the south. "There was a blue boat that raced through the other morning, kind of low in the water. Looked like he had something covered with blue tarps. When he came back through, whatever he was covering up was gone, and he was light, racing along like the devil was after him."

"A blue boat. I don't suppose you saw his registration number or any special markings?"

"He was too far away and going too fast to see anything except the tarp and the guy. I only remember it because most people aren't in that big a rush, and he was pushing so much water going south that he really rocked our boat."

"So, he didn't hang around like he was fishing?"

"Now you mention it, he didn't even have any fishing rods," the guy in the back remarked.

"Tell me about the boat. Was it light blue? Dark blue? Long? Short? Anything special about it?"

"It was kinda sparkling blue, and it looked too shallow to be out in a storm, like a bass boat. Most of the boats out here have a deeper hull. You want to have a little freeboard if the wind comes up."

"Thanks. Good luck!" I pushed the bow away, and Jill pushed the stern. We motored slowly back to the main channel.

"Do you think you got a solid lead out of them?"

"I'm not sure. They spent a lot of time looking at each other like they really didn't want to tell me what they'd seen."

104

"You're way too cynical. I've seen that happen a lot with older park visitors. They like to wait to see if the other person is going to answer first. I always assumed it was because they were hard of hearing and hoped the other person better understood the question."

I considered her remarks, and they seemed reasonable. "There are probably a million sparkly blue bass boats in Texas."

"Not in the ocean or the bay. Like they said, they're not built for rough water. And, now you know that they're coming down from CC."

"The old guy in the back of the boat was checking out your cleavage when you pushed away."

Jill laughed. "I hope he got an eyeful. Describing my décolletage as cleavage is an overstatement."

"You made an old man's day."

Jill shook her head but was smiling.

We continued slowly down the channel, Jill sitting on a cushion on top of a cooler and me behind the wheel. We spooked some ducks, saw a few fish jump, and enjoyed the uncluttered scenery along the waterway.

"What's Rachel doing this morning without you?"

"I warned her I was taking the boat out again this morning. She's driving the beach."

"You should bring her along on this tour. I bet she'd enjoy the change of scenery."

I sensed the whine of a high-speed motor coming through the boat hull more than through the air. I shifted into neutral and shut off the motor. Jill looked at me with an unasked question in her eyes.

"Do you hear the motor?"

"I hear something." The whine became louder, now audible behind us.

I pulled a pair of binoculars out of a storage compartment and looked behind us. I could see the prow of a boat and the white froth of its wake coming down the middle of the channel. I handed Jill the binoculars, restarted the motor, and eased the vessel out of the main channel. It took almost a minute for the boat to reach us. The huge twin Mercury outboard motors screamed like they were running at full throttle, but he wasn't flying past.

"He's got a blue tarp covering something in the center of the boat." Jill assessed through the binoculars. "It's your blue boat. It looks like there's just one guy in it. He's wearing wraparound sunglasses and a backward baseball cap."

"Get out your phone and see if you can get a picture of the boat and registration number when he passes." I eased the throttle ahead and steered in the same direction he traveled. Jill pulled her phone out of her pocket and quickly paged through the apps to open the camera, then leaned toward the channel, keeping the phone low so it wouldn't be obvious she was taking a photo.

The man glanced at us but seemed unconcerned. Having Jill in a boat bristling with fishing poles provided enough camouflage that he blew past without a second look. I turned the boat so our bow faced toward his wake and eased the throttle ahead.

The white wake rolled toward us. Jill stuffed her phone back into her pocket and grabbed the cooler handles. The bow rose, then quickly fell, pitching Jill up, then down again. She lost her grip and rolled off the cooler. I gripped the steering wheel with both hands and bent my knees, managing to keep myself upright.

"What a thoughtless bastard." Jill pulled herself back atop the cooler. She brushed sand off her shorts and arms.

I eased the throttle ahead until at maximum. The blue boat was a hundred yards ahead of us by the time I got to the middle of the channel. Even at top speed, the FW&S boat was falling behind.

I picked up the radio mic. "Coast Guard, Coast Guard. This is the Park Service requesting assistance."

"Park Service, meet me on twenty-two."

I switched the channel. "Coast Guard, this is the Park Service. I'm in Laguna Madre following a boat I suspect is carrying toxic chemicals. Do you have anyone who can render assistance?"

"Park Service, this is the Coast Guard station in Corpus Christi Bay. Our helo is south of your location and providing support to the Naval Air Station operations today, and both our boats in the bay are in the Port Aransas area. I can't get anyone to you soon. Are you in danger?"

"There is no physical threat. We're in pursuit of a blue bass boat we suspect is carrying pails of toxic waste. We'll continue our pursuit."

"Roger that, Park Service. I'll notify the CCPD. Their boat may be available to assist you."

"I'll be back on sixteen."

Jill had picked up the binoculars while I was on the radio and was watching the other boat, quickly fading from view. "I don't think he's concerned about us. He never even turned around to look back. Can you go any faster?"

I adjusted the motor's trim, which put it at a slightly different angle. We gained a little speed, but not enough to keep up with the blue boat. "That's the best I can do."

We continued to race down the waterway, but quickly lost sight of the other boat and soon even its wake disappeared. Jill scanned the shoreline ahead while I focused on the channel to not run the boat aground in the shallows or "spoil piles" that had been dredged up by the Corps of Engineers.

"There! On the left!" Jill pointed down the channel. "He's beached the boat." She looked through the binoculars again. "He's tossing pails onto shore."

Our approach seemed painfully slow, and he worked fast. I could see the man clearly, but he had finished his dumping and was backing the boat away from shore. We were still more than a hundred yards away. He spun the boat around, coming back toward us. In a few seconds, his boat was up "on plane" and flying toward us at what must've been fifty miles-an-hour.

"Grab the shotgun out of the storage locker," I shouted to be heard over the motor. When we were about fifty yards apart, I cut the motor and spun the wheel, so we were broadside in the channel and drifting to a stop. I waved my arms to slow him down. When it became clear he wasn't planning to stop, I grabbed the shotgun and pointed it at him.

The boat was upon us in seconds, and as soon as the driver saw the shotgun, he ducked behind the capstan, then turned hard to the left as he got closer. The huge wave he pushed up rolled toward us as fast as his boat. No one was in mortal danger, so I knew I couldn't use deadly force, but I fired the proverbial "shot over his bow," hoping he'd slow or stop. Instead, he fishtailed, throwing up even more wake, then barreled past before I could pump the shotgun.

"Look out!" Jill yelled as the massive wake rolled into the side of our boat. She threw herself to the deck, and I grabbed for the steering wheel but missed. I let go of the shotgun a fraction of a second before I was thrown against the opposite gunwale. The railing cut my knees out from under me, and I had the sensation of flying for a second before I hit the water.

I was disoriented when I came up. The orange life jacket pushed my neck and shoulders up, but the water running off my head blinded me. I had the terrible thought the boat might've been swamped. Then I heard Jill yell my name.

"I'm here." I wiped the water from my eyes and saw her standing at the gunwale, holding out a pole. She pulled me to the boat, and after a bit of swimming and pulling, I got to the motor where I could place my foot on something solid and step over the transom. In the boat, I bent down to catch my breath.

"Are you okay?" Jill had her hand on my back.

"Yeah. I think I bruised my ego, but that's it." A sudden panic attack rushed through me, and I reached for my hip. My holster was still there, as were my badge, wallet, and handcuffs. "The shotgun?"

"You dropped it before you went over the side. It's right over there, on the deck."

"Let's catch the guy," I said, stepping up to the capstan.

"He's long gone. He disappeared while you were still in the water."

I picked up the radio mic. "Coast Guard, this is the Park Service. Meet me on twenty-two." I switched the radio channel.

"Go ahead, Park Service."

"The boat we were observing tried to swamp us. We're not in danger, but he's racing up the Laguna Madre toward Corpus Christi at high speed."

"We've still got no one near you. Do you have a description or identification of the boat?"

"What's your picture look like?" I asked Jill.

She grabbed her phone and pulled up the pictures. They were blurry like they'd been smeared with mud.

"We have no description other than a blue bass boat operated by a single white male operator wearing wraparound sunglasses and a red baseball cap backward on his head."

"Got that. I'll notify all law enforcement in the area and hail the wharf operators to have them be on watch."

"Thanks, Coast Guard."

Jill flipped through the pictures on her phone. She held it up for me. "I got three pictures, and this is the best." The picture she showed me had a good view of the man operating the boat, but there was nothing that would give us the identity of the boat or the operator. I couldn't even determine his hair color because of his cap.

"Shit," I said.

"What's your plan?"

"I want to chase the guy, but I know that'd be fruitless. Let's motor down to where he was dumping."

Finding the dumpsite wasn't as easy as I thought it would be. We cruised up and down the waterway in the area Jill thought she'd seen the boat beached. She studied the shoreline with the binoculars while I navigated through the water to stay deep enough to protect the motor.

"There!" she yelled, pointing toward shore.

I spun the wheel and tilted the motor to go through the shallower water. She leaned on the front gunwale, directing me around hazards in the water, but moving toward the area where she'd spotted the dumped pails on the shore. I finally saw the bright blue of a bucket and homed in on the spot. I cut the motor when we were about twenty feet from shore. Jill jumped over the side when the water was only inches deep, and she pulled the boat onto the shore.

She struggled to move her feet in the mucky bottom. "You could've warned me the bottom was mud."

"Sorry. I was focused on the pails."

I jumped off and pulled the boat onto shore. The pails were in a depression no more than four feet from the waterline. They were dented and jumbled together, but no smell emanated from the pile, as had come from the previous site where several of the pails had popped open or cracked. We walked around the heap.

"Why did he paint over the labels?" Jill asked.

"We can't trace the source or contents. It makes the investigation much harder."

"Are we taking some pails back with us?"

"I don't want to risk handling any of this without knowing how toxic, flammable, or radioactive the contents are."

"Radioactive? Really?"

"If it's medical waste, it may be some radioisotopes for diagnosis or treatment of cancer. I just don't want to endanger anyone by moving it around. I'll put a waypoint into the GPS, so we can find this spot again and bring in the cleanup crew. Let's go."

I gestured for Jill to get into the boat. "Ladies first."

"You get in. Go to the back. Your weight will lift the bow out of the muck. I'll give us a push and hopefully not lose a shoe in the muck."

"You're so smart," I said as I climbed over the bow.

"And you're so full of it." I felt the bow slide as Jill gave us a push. She hopped over the bow like a gymnast.

It took us half an hour to get back to the fishermen. They waved frantically as we approached. I eased the boat next to them.

"What's up?" I asked as they caught our boat.

"Did you see that guy in the blue boat?" The man with the patch over his ear asked.

"Yeah, we followed him down the waterway. He's the person we want."

"Why didn't you arrest him?" the man in the stern asked.

"His motor was faster. We couldn't catch him."

"We heard a shot."

"I shot across his bow, and it didn't slow him down."

Jill smiled. "You realize you're going to have to fill out a firearm discharge report."

"I suppose I would if there had been a witness."

"We could be your witnesses," the man in the front said, looking hopeful.

I shook my head. "That's okay. We've got it covered."

"I don't suppose you got any identification off the boat," Jill asked.

The man in the front shook his head. "We've both got cataracts, so we miss a lot."

"The way you were waving I thought maybe you'd seen something."

"Naw." The man with the ear patch shook his head. "We were kind of concerned about you. We wanted to make sure you were okay."

"Thanks."

They stepped away from the gunwale, watching Jill, and waited for us to push off. I put my heel on their boat and pushed, and we started to drift away. Jill waved, without leaning over the gunwale to push off. The men were visibly disappointed.

"Did you see that? They were just waiting for me to lean over so they'd get an eyeful."

"Can't say I blame them." My comment garnered a glare, followed by a headshake and grin. I turned the up the channel toward the Park Service boat launch.

"What's your plan, Doug?"

"I don't have one."

"I could call the marinas while you drive the beach this afternoon. The blue boat might be moored somewhere along the bay."

"You're on leave."

"As you pointed out, I'm being paid, I still have a badge and the Park Superintendent title."

"I thought you were enjoying your time off." I slowed as we approached the launch area. A fisherman with a medium-sized boat was backing his trailer down the ramp. We idled while he took the boat off the trailer and tied it to the dock.

"I am enjoying Texas, but I get a little restless. It's more stressful not having a daily agenda than I expected. I've had my days programmed since I was in kindergarten. I had to get up, eat breakfast, catch the bus, spend my day in school, then bus home, eat supper. Later years, there was homework in the evenings. I went to college, and my life was more freeform, but there was still the structure of classes and studying. Work had structure. Suddenly, the structure is gone. As odd as it sounds, it's stressful not to have the phone ringing and people knocking on my door."

"Retired people get used to that. I'm sure you'll adapt."

"Just the same, it'd be fun to make a few calls about the blue boat. I'm invested in the chase now and I'd like to do that. Are you okay with me calling around?"

The pickup with the trailer pulled away, and I motored to the dock. Jill jumped onto the pier and tied us off while I shut down and tilted the motor.

It took a few minutes to back the trailer down the launch, then to talk with the boater who was curious about my badge, gun, and the shotgun in the boat. I pulled the boat out, strapped it down securely, and pulled the drain plug before pulling out of the parking lot.

"You didn't answer my question. Are you okay with me making some calls?"

"I have to give you points for persistence. Most people take the hint when I drop a topic."

"Listen, Fletcher, I'd like to think of us as partners. If I'm your partner, no topic is off-limits, and questions get answers."

"Partners? I thought we were lovers."

"Either way, the same rules apply. Unless you want to change our arrangement." She stared at me, waiting for an answer.

"Don't get your undies in a bunch." As soon as the words were out of my mouth, I regretted them.

"Don't get my undies in a bunch! Really! I'm just supposed to sit quietly and let you brood over things and blow off my questions? That's not how I work, and if that's how you need things to be, I can pack my stuff and book a flight back to Arizona."

"I'm sorry. That was a poor choice of words."

"And?"

"And, I don't want you to pack up or leave."

"So, we're partners?"

We turned onto the highway going to Port Aransas while I considered my response.

"We've both been living alone for a long time, and it's going to take a while for us to figure out how our lives mesh. I want to figure that out, but there are going to be a few rough spots. I want you to be part of my life, and I absolutely love the parts we've sorted out and found common ground."

"You like me cooking your meals, washing your clothes, kissing you when you come home from work, and the sex. I'm not here to be your concubine or housekeeper."

"I like having you in my life. I'd be just fine if you never cooked another meal or washed another load of my clothes. I have to admit the bedroom part is pretty spectacular."

"I accept your apology." She reached across the seat and squeezed my hand.

"I didn't apologize. I was just explaining how I felt."

"I take it as an apology. Let it go. Okay?"

"Go ahead and make some calls but be careful. Don't go chasing after this case alone. The people involved in this are dumping because it's saving them a lot of money, and people with lots of money on the line can be dangerous."

"Yes, mister ranger, sir."

"I'm serious! I don't want you to get mixed up in something dangerous."

"Okay. I get it. Are we okay? I think we just had a fight."

"That was hardly a fight. Nobody swore, and no dishes were broken."

Jill touched my cheek. "I take it you and your ex had some knockdown battles."

"There were a couple. Mostly, we had a frosty relationship where there wasn't much communication other than glares and slamming doors."

"That's not my style. I like things out on the table and dealt with. If you feel something, say it out loud. Don't go skulking around making me guess why you're mad."

"Okay. I love you. I'm putting it on the table for discussion." I looked at Jill, who was staring out the side window. "The street of open discussion runs both directions."

"It's too soon," she said without turning away from the window.

"Why is it too soon?"

She turned toward me, and tears welled in her eyes. "I don't believe in love at first sight, and I don't believe you're ready for someone like me. You're ruggedly handsome, and I'm a tomboy. You still turn women's heads when you walk through the supermarket. You may not notice it, but I do. I don't feel…"

"You don't feel what? You don't feel love?"

"I'd love for you to be in love with me. But I don't feel…worthy."

I was stunned. I turned off the highway and into the lot behind the townhouses. I backed the boat trailer into an open spot and turned off the pickup.

Jill reached to unbuckle her seatbelt, and I grabbed her hand. "You're my best friend. Can you accept that?"

"I guess."

"I've never been closer to a woman in my life than I am to you. Beyond my deep respect and friendship, you fill a place in my heart no one else has ever been."

"Okay."

"Tell me how you feel."

"I can't."

"Why not?"

"I feel like a schoolgirl with her first crush. I feel butterflies when I see you. I've never felt this way before, and it scares the hell out of me because I can't believe you're feeling the same things."

She pulled her hand free, unbuckled the seatbelt, and climbed out of the pickup. By the time I got to the trailer, she'd already unhooked the safety chains and released the hitch. I unhooked the light harness and cranked down the wheel. I unloaded the shotgun, while she carried the fishing rods into the house. We set the gear in the entry closet and bumped shoulders.

Jill sniffed my shirt. "You need a shower. You smell like a swamp."

"Come along. Take a shower with me."

"That's not going to happen."

"It might be fun."

"Uh-uh. Not happening."

I pulled her close and kissed her. "I feel those same things. I feel the butterflies, and I feel undeserving of your love."

"You're just trying to get me into the shower."

"I'm going to work and getting you into the shower or bed isn't part of that plan." I walked up the stairs, piled fresh clothes on the bed, and walked into the bathroom. I could smell the swampy odor when the water washed over my head, so I lathered with shampoo twice and scrubbed my skin until it turned pink. Jill was leaning against the sink when I stepped out of the shower.

"I field-stripped and oiled your Sig while you were showering. There was a minnow stuck between the second and third rounds in the magazine."

"You're kidding," I said as I toweled off.

"I'm kidding about the minnow, but I did field-strip and clean your weapon."

I pulled on underwear, then stepped over to the sink and kissed her. "I don't think there are a dozen women in the world who would do that for a guy."

"Maybe it's my way of saying I'm sorry for being bitchy."

I pulled on the fresh khaki pants and a brown golf shirt. The Sig was back in the holster, sitting next to my badge and handcuffs, all on top of a newspaper spread on the bed. The dirty clothes I'd dropped carelessly on the bathroom floor were gone. "I would've put the clothes in the hamper."

"I was afraid you'd stink up everything in there. I put them right into the washer."

"If that doesn't say, 'I love you,' I don't know what does." I kissed her and clipped the holster to my belt. She stood with her arms crossed and head cocked. "What?" I asked.

Tears glistened in her eyes. "We're not having this discussion while you're dashing out the door. Go to the park. I'll pull something together for supper."

Chapter 10

Wednesday afternoon

The radio crackled to life. "This is Coast Guard helicopter hailing the Park Service. Does anyone copy?"

Rachel picked up the mic. "This is the Park Service. Meet on twenty-two." She flipped the channel and keyed the mic. "Hi, Bruce. What've you got?"

I saw the orange and white Coast Guard helicopter hovering over the shoreline ahead of us.

"Is that you in the pickup coming down the shore?"

"Ten-four."

"We've got something in the water that requires your attention."

"Can you explain?"

"Not over the radio."

"Can you stay on station until we get there?"

"We're at your beck and call unless something more pressing arises."

Rachel hung the mic on the dashboard bracket.

"Do you get called by the Coast Guard very often?" I asked.

"The correct terminology is, we were hailed."

"Hailed?"

"That's maritime jargon for someone contacting us. Everyone monitors channel sixteen."

"Do you know Bruce socially?"

"We try to meet all the local law enforcement people. I visited the Coast Guard station and got to know most of the pilots and crews. Didn't you do that in Minnesota?"

"We stayed close to the county deputies and the U.S. Marshals. They're the ones we ran into most often on joint operations and in emergencies."

"No Feds other than the Marshals?"

"We stumbled across the FBI, DEA and Homeland Security in a few operations, but I wouldn't characterize my relationship with the other Feds as cordial."

"I heard about you and the FBI in Flagstaff. Saying they weren't your friends would seem to be an understatement."

"My friends don't cut me out of joint investigations, then take credit for solving the crime at a news conference."

"Ouch!"

"I don't have a lot of time for the FBI." We'd covered the miles to the helicopter quickly, and Rachel slowed as I studied the water being whipped up under the helicopter's wash. "It's a body."

"What kind of body?" Rachel asked, studying the surface.

"Human."

"I got that part. What's it doing here?"

"Floating."

"Can you be serious, Doug?"

The radio came to life. "Park Service. Do you require any further assistance?"

I picked up the mic. "We've got it. Thanks for the assist."

The helicopter responded by clicking the mic twice, then they circled once then turned down the coast.

Rachel stopped the pickup on the packed sand just beyond the reach of the waves. "Why did you let them go? They might've been willing to put their swimmer down to bring the body ashore."

"You don't think we can recover it ourselves?"

The body rolled with the gentle ocean swells. The bulging bloated white abdomen was the most prominent feature.

"How are you planning to handle this?" she asked.

I got out of the truck, took off my gun belt, and laid it on the passenger side floor of the cab. "One of us has to wade out and pull him ashore."

"Hang on. What makes you say, 'him?'" she asked as I took off my shoes and socks.

"That's not a periscope sticking up below his swollen abdomen."

"I've got a degree in biology. You can use technical terms, like penis, without offending me." She paused. "Why's it sticking up?"

"When the body starts to decompose, gases collect inside the peritoneum, which causes the body to float. As the pressure builds, the abdomen becomes bloated, and it puts pressure in every direction making his penis stick out, and that's how I knew it was a man."

"Put your shoes back on. I've got this." Rachel climbed out of the truck and took off her shoes.

"You're serious?"

"You said I've got to learn to be a cop someday, and this is apparently part of the job. Do you have any suggestions on how to do this?"

"Take off your gun and duty belt."

She pulled off her shoes and unbuckled her belt. She wrapped the belt around her holster and handcuffs, then set them on the driver's seat. "Any other suggestions?"

"I was going to take off my pants and wade out in my underwear."

"That's not happening." She gave me a look as if unsure I was kidding or serious, then she waded into the water, pausing when the water hit her waist. She raised up on her toes when the next swell hit her. The water rose to her ribs, and her light gray shirt turned dark from the soaking. She reached out and grabbed one of the man's fingers and pulled him toward shore. After she'd only taken a couple steps, a large swell picked up the body and threw it against her. The force knocked her over, then washed him over the top of her. She came up gasping, frantically pushing the body away from her. To her credit, she didn't scream or run but grabbed the man's hand and kept pulling. I waded out knee-deep, grabbing the man's other hand. He became heavy when we dragged his torso onto the sand.

The decomposition smell assaulted me when I knelt down to examine the corpse. "Have you got some rubber gloves in the truck?" I asked as I stood.

Rachel shook the water from her hands and picked a piece of seaweed from her pants. "I think there are gloves in the first aid kit."

I reached behind the pickup seat and took out a first aid kit. There were a handful of purple nitrile gloves, I pulled on a pair and took a pair to Rachel.

We each grabbed one of John Doe's wrists, and together, we dragged him above the waterline.

Rachel stared at the waxy corpse. His eyes were open, but already milky. "Why'd you get the gloves? Don't you think it's a little late to try and preserve evidence?"

"It's not to preserve evidence. It's to protect you from the smell that's permeating your skin."

She sniffed her hands. "You could've given me the gloves before I waded out."

"Sorry. It just occurred to me when we pulled the body ashore."

I knelt down and looked at the body. "He's been dead long enough for rigor mortis to relax, but there's no sign he's been in the surf a long time. There isn't significant abrasion to his hands, and the ocean critters haven't nibbled on his fingers and toes. His eyes are milky blue. His wrists and ankles are still bound with plastic cable ties cutting deeply into the flesh, but it looks like other restraints have been cut to free his arms and legs."

"What's with his neck?"

The throat had been cut ear-to-ear, and his tongue pulled out through the gash. "That's called a Jamaican necktie."

Rachel's face turned ashen, and she spun around and fell to her knees. Her stomach contents splashed onto the sand as she gagged. It took her a few minutes on her knees before she rolled over and sat on the sand, wiping her mouth on her forearm. She looked at me like she expected me to comment then crossed her legs. "That wasn't very professional."

"Cut yourself some slack. Most cops toss their cookies at their first murder scene."

"Do you think he was killed on a boat and dumped overboard?"

"It's best not to jump to conclusions until the evidence comes in." I picked up one hand and examined the fingers. "He put up a fight before he died."

"How can you tell?"

127

"His fingernails are broken." I held the hand up so Rachel could see. She glanced at the hand, but her eyes quickly returned to the gash on the man's neck.

"Why did you call that a Jamaican necktie?"

"I saw reports of this type of wound coming out of Jamaica when I was in St. Paul. It spread through the Jamaican gangs in the U.S. It signifies shutting up someone. The Asian gangs use it on police informants."

"This guy is Caucasian. He's not the member of an Asian or Jamaican gang."

"I don't see a tattoo anywhere. I doubt he's a gang member or a convict." I paused. "Do you have a plastic tarp in the truck?"

"There's a toolbox in the back. There's supposed to be a tarp inside unless someone used it and didn't replace it."

I found the tarp, carried it back to the body, and laid it out on the sand. "Let's roll him onto the tarp. He'll slide better over the sand on the plastic. Then we can use it to lift him into the back of the pickup."

Rachel nodded her assent and stood up. We rolled him onto his face. The pressure on his abdomen caused gas to push out of his stomach, making a gurgling belching sound. Rachel's eyes went wide, and she stepped back, letting go of the tarp.

"Gas," I said.

"Is that natural?"

"It's common when the body has been decomposing for a while."

It was a struggle for the two of us to get the body onto the tailgate.

"Why don't you wring out your cuffs on the driver's side of the pickup, Doug. I'm going to wring out my uniform by the tailgate. It's not like it'll dry in this humidity, but I can at least get it to stop dripping."

I wrung out my pants cuffs as best I could, brushed most of the sand off my feet, then put my socks and shoes on. I set Rachel's holster on the dash and got in the driver's door. I considered calling in our location, but I didn't want to broadcast the recovery of a murder victim over the maritime hailing channel. Motion in the passenger's mirror caught my eye. Rachel was wringing out her pants and shirt. She was slender to the point of being skinny. She stood next to the fender wearing a lacy red bra and thong, which explained why she'd been unwilling to strip her pants off before wading into the surf. I looked away, but not before she glanced at the mirror and our eyes met.

She climbed back into the pickup and moved her gun belt and shoes to the floor. Her clothes were more than damp and badly wrinkled from being wrung out.

"Are you okay?" I asked, putting the pickup into gear.

"Pretty much," she replied. "I wish you'd suggested I take my cellphone out of my pocket when you told me to take off my shoes and gun." She set a white iPhone on the seat between us. The screen was dark.

"If you'd taken off your pants…"

"Yeah. Yeah. That didn't happen, and it's too late to go back. Maybe if I pack the phone in rice overnight, it'll dry out."

"I hate to be a naysayer, but I don't think cellphones survive immersion in seawater."

"At this point, I've got nothing to lose but a pound of raw rice."

I dug the cellphone out of my pocket and handed it to her. "Call Matt and tell him to notify the coroner or medical examiner."

* * *

An ambulance was parked in front of the visitor center with its blue lights flashing when we drove off the beach. Matt stood near the front fender with the two ambulance attendants. A small crowd had gathered near them on the sidewalk. I parked the pickup next to the ambulance and left the keys in the ignition.

I walked over and leaned close to Matt. "We don't need an ambulance."

"It's the county protocol," he whispered. "The ambulance crew can declare the victim dead, then transport him to the hospital morgue."

Rachel and the EMTs hopped onto the pickup bed. One of the EMTs took the stethoscope off his neck and listened briefly, then draped it back over his neck. The two

EMTs and Rachel spoke for a moment then hopped off the tailgate with the agility of the young. I would've been much less graceful.

Matt carefully stayed clear of the back of the pickup. "You're sure the victim is dead?"

Rachel and the ambulance crew carefully wrapped the body in the blue tarp.

"He hasn't been with us for at least a day or two." I looked at the gathering crowd of gawkers. "Okay, folks. Please step back." I put my arms wide, and Matt followed my lead, moving the onlookers further away from the ambulance. Rachel and the EMTs slid John Doe onto their gurney and then loaded the tarp wrapped body into the ambulance.

Rachel, Matt, and I watched the ambulance drive away.

Matt nodded toward the building. "Let's go to my office." We walked to his office, and he closed the door behind us. Rachel and I sat in the gray metal chairs with matching gray vinyl seats, which must be Park Service standard issue because they were identical to the ones in Jill's Flagstaff office. Matt sat in his desk chair that creaked like it needed a drop of oil. "You two have had quite a day."

"I assume you don't get dead bodies every day," I said.

Matt shook his head. "We've never had one before, but they seem to show up when you do, Doug."

"I can assure you I had nothing to do with this."

"Rachel, you look like you slept in your uniform."

"I waded out to recover the body, then I wrung out my clothes, so I didn't soak the pickup seats."

"Doug, do you have any thoughts about the body? I mean, do you think he fell off a ship?"

"There's no way to tell where he came from. If you're worried that he might've died on Park Service property, I'd say the odds are slim. You control access, so it's not like someone drove past the gatehouse and dumped a body next to the visitor center. I imagine he was dropped overboard somewhere offshore, or he drifted down the shore with the current."

"Doug said the gash in his neck and the lolling tongue are characteristic of a gang trying to make a statement about a snitch or informant." Rachel readily gave me credit for my observations, which raised her in my esteem.

Matt shook his head. "I'll have to call the Park Service regional office. I assume there are forms to fill out. Is there anything else we need to do, Doug?"

"I'd like to attend the autopsy. That'll give us a better idea of where John Doe came from, and whether it's a case we need to follow or if it's someone else's investigation."

Matt stood, signaling the end of our discussion. "Doug, I'm glad you were here to help us deal with this. I wouldn't know where to begin, and I suspect the other agencies who will get involved would bowl us right over. Right, Rachel?"

"I'm not sure I could've even got the body out of the surf without Doug."

I smiled. "It would've been a lift, but you would've managed."

"No, I don't think I would've had the nerve to wade out and make the recovery without your encouragement."

"It's a good thing you were partners today." Matt slapped my shoulder and patted Rachel on the back.

Rachel smiled as we walked away. "I was wrong about you. I thought you'd be an arrogant asshole. You're not arrogant; you're confident."

"That's quite a compliment."

"Would you like to come over for supper sometime? Toby makes a super vegan chili."

I smiled, but the thought of vegan chili left me cold. "I'd like that. Can I bring Jill?"

"Please bring her over. I'd like to meet the person who is in love with a crusty old cop who can drag a body out of the ocean without getting sick." Rachel paused. "Thanks again for being there today. I'm seriously not sure what I'd have done without you."

"You did okay, for a rookie,"

"And, you're a real gentleman."

"I am?"

"I saw you glance at me in the mirror while I was wringing out my clothes. You looked away rather than leering. That's being a gentleman."

"I'm sorry…"

"I could've stood behind the tailgate. But when you looked away and kept your eyes off the mirrors, I knew you weren't a creepy old man."

"I guess I'm too much of a Boy Scout to be a voyeur."

"Were you an Eagle Scout?"

I nodded.

"You might just have disproven one of my stereotypes. I thought Eagle Scouts were a myth perpetuated by the good old boys. Maybe it really does mean something."

"The Eagle badge is something that took a lot of effort and commitment when I was a fourteen-year-old kid. I'd like to think it means something."

Rachel considered my words for a while. "I'll talk to Toby and see when he's willing to whip up a batch of chili."

Chapter 11

I mulled John Doe's discovery and Rachel's comments about Eagle scouts on my drive down Mustang Island. I passed under a bridge as a golf cart whizzed overhead, racing toward the few green golf holes on the west side of the highway, breaking up the monotonous brown on the bayside of the highway. I drove a Park Service pickup with an emergency light bar mounted on top. Driving only slightly over the speed limit caused a string of cars to back up behind me. A few seemed tempted to pass but pulled back into the flow when they saw the pickup's light bar.

I hit a stoplight at the first gas station/convenience store in the twelve-mile drive. The left road led to a development of small mansions built along canals dredged from the pastureland. The structures had been decimated by the hurricane, and there were dozens of construction trucks lining the narrow streets. I turned east, toward the Gulf, and drove through a residential neighborhood with less hurricane damage. A few houses had been demolished, leaving a checkerboard of empty lots, houses under repair, stilt houses, and

135

cement block houses that had withstood the hurricane.

The townhouse door was unlocked. When I walked in, my nose was met by the delicious aroma of garlic, onions, and baking bread.

Jill looked around the corner. "I'm going to put the fish in the cioppino. It'll be ready as soon as you change clothes."

I put my clothes into the laundry hamper and showered, scrubbing hard to get rid of the dead body smell. I pulled on a golf shirt I'd won as a door prize at a St. Paul Police golf fundraiser and a pair of shorts then headed downstairs to the kitchen.

Jill had set the table and poured glasses of red wine. She put a pot on a trivet in the center of the table and ladled dinner into our bowls. There was a basket of steaming bread with bottles of balsamic vinegar and olive oil next to it. The whole dinner looked sumptuous, and Jill beamed. She wore tan cargo shorts and a pink tank top. Between her smile, personal energy, and outfit, she looked ten years younger than when we'd left Arizona.

I froze for a second, looking at her hair. "I like your haircut." I knew the correct response, regardless of my opinion. The short hairdo made her look younger.

"I decided the long hair and ponytail were too hot for Texas. I had the beauty shop cut it short and add some blonde highlights. I'm glad you like it." She fluffed it and turned her head like she was posing for a magazine.

"It makes you look younger."

"There was a lot of gray hair on the floor when they finished."

"I'd never seen a corkscrew." I sipped wine, avoiding the gray hair topic.

"It's in the drawer with the vegetable peeler you'd probably never seen."

"I haven't peeled any carrots."

"That's cioppino in your bowl." She unfolded a paper napkin and set it on her lap. "Pour a little balsamic vinegar onto your plate, then add some olive oil to dip the French bread."

"Is the grocery store nearby?"

"It's just a couple blocks across the highway. I also found a fabulous fish market. Taste the cioppino. It has fresh shrimp, scallops, and snapper."

I swallowed a spoonful of the broth and was amazed at the rich flavors.

"Scoop up a scallop or shrimp."

I scooped up a shrimp and blew on it for a few seconds. She sipped wine while I waited for the shrimp to cool. When I bit down, I realized I'd never had shrimp like it before, mild, tender, and sweet. "That's even better than the shrimp we had with Matt and Mandy. And the wine is excellent. Where'd you find it?"

"I found a bottle in the clearance cart at the grocery store. Apparently, Texans aren't into Argentine Malbec. I hope you like it because I bought several bottles."

"How was bridge?" I sipped wine, dipped bread, and ate cioppino.

"It was more intense than I remembered. I think my grandma's friends accepted that I was a novice and taught me as we played. The bridge group expected me to bid properly and keep track of which cards had been played. It took a few hands before I got back into it. I felt bad for the woman who got stuck being my partner, but she was understanding and talked me through some of the errors I made. We won the last game, so that made up for some of my earlier play."

"It sounds a little stressful," I said.

"They said they'd call me when they needed someone to fill in, so I must've been okay by the time we got to the end."

"What did you do after bridge?"

"I called a couple of marinas. None of the local fishermen use bass boats."

"You're at a dead end?"

"I'll make a few more calls before I give up, but it doesn't look promising."

"That was your afternoon?"

Jill shook her head as she chewed. "I walked all over downtown Port Aransas. I went a different gym next to the hairstylist and started a ten-day free trial. I checked out a couple of tourist traps and found some beach clothes on sale, bought a cookbook at a half-price bookstore, bought the seafood for the cioppino recipe, and then I cooked supper." She rattled off the activities of her day rapid-fire, like someone who'd just discovered Disneyland. She seemed almost giddy, and I glanced at the wine bottle to see if she'd been sipping wine while she had been cooking.

"No, I wasn't drinking while I was cooking." She chewed on a piece of crusty bread and took a sip of wine. "I feel like the weight of the world has been lifted off my shoulders. I didn't realize how the Flagstaff stress had gotten to me. Being able to make a couple calls, then focus on shopping and making supper was such an indulgent gift to myself, I felt guilty for a while. Then I said, '*To hell with it!*' I'm not going to let the past drag me down."

I smiled and held up my wine glass. "How about a toast to Texas and new beginnings." We touched glasses and took a sip.

"How was your day?"

"We recovered a body from the surf."

Jill stopped eating and stared at me. "Was it a swimmer who drowned?"

"I doubt it. It was a naked guy who'd been in the water a while. The Corpus Christi Medical Examiner got the body."

"That's a hell of a welcome to a new job."

"Matt assured me this was an anomaly. They haven't ever had a body wash ashore before, at least not as far as he knows."

"How did you find it. I mean, were you driving the beach and then saw him in the surf?"

"The Coast Guard called it in. They patrol the coastline, and one of their helicopters spotted the body in the water and guided us to the location."

"You had to wade out to recover him?"

"I didn't."

"You made the young female ranger wade into the surf to recover a naked body?"

"I thought it would be tacky for me to strip down to my underwear and wade into the surf while my young female partner watched."

"That's sexist."

"I'm kidding. Rachel volunteered."

"Rachel volunteered to wade out for the body?"

"She did."

"How did she handle it?"

"It went okay until the wave threw the body against her and knocked her down."

Jill dove back into her dinner. "Oh, God, I can picture it."

"You're getting as hardened and cynical as me. You kept eating."

Jill sopped up the last of the cioppino broth with a piece of bread, then washed it down with a swallow of wine. "When somebody's dead, they're dead. If I haven't tried to save them, or if it's not a kid, I can compartmentalize the event. It helps that I never saw the body. It's just an abstraction."

"It was pretty gross. I think Rachel is going to have some trouble falling asleep tonight."

"She'll have a touch of PTSD?"

"Maybe. She's growing as a cop and dealing with the body took her a long way down that pathway." I loaded the dishwasher. "Let's take a walk on the beach."

Jill smiled. "You just passed test number three."

"I guess I missed tests one and two."

She ticked items off on her fingers. "You picked up your dirty clothes and put them in the laundry hamper and you didn't leave the toilet lid open. Now you're loading the dishwasher without being asked. If you learn to replace the toilet paper, I'll declare you housebroken."

"I know how to change toilet paper. I was in a hurry."

"It only takes ten seconds, dear."

I kissed her. "You're going to keep me around for a while?"

"I think so."

* * *

We walked to the beach as cars and pickups streamed out of the parking lot. The sun was setting over Corpus Christi bay, and only a few die-hard teens were catching the last rays of sun on the Gulf side. The sand was packed hard from the surf and the tires that had driven over it, making the walk easy. Lights from the offshore drilling platforms twinkled above the surface of the water.

Jill grabbed my hand and intertwined her fingers with mine. "I've been thinking about the conversation we started this morning. I know I'm still on vacation, but I like it here. The

141

people in the stores are friendly and polite. They have a drawl, but they act like Midwesterners. The pace of life is a little slower than Arizona, but I think I could get used to this."

"Are you telling me you'll stay here, even if you can return to your old job?"

"I honestly don't know. I guess I'm saying this is a nice, comfortable place. It could be home under the right circumstances."

I pulled her close and kissed the top of her head. "Rachel wants us to come over for supper sometime. She's going to check dates with her boyfriend."

"Have you ever done this much socializing?"

"Not unless getting drunk in a bar with a bunch of cops counts."

"I suppose that's one form of socializing. I wondered if you'd socialized with a mixed group and had a polite conversation like we did with Matt and Mandy."

"It's been a while." I tried to remember if that had ever happened in the years I'd been married.

"You got quiet."

"Like you said, this is a new chapter. Let's leave the old ones behind."

Chapter 12

Thursday Morning

Matt was in his office with a pile of papers on his desk. He looked annoyed when I knocked, but the annoyance quickly melted away when he saw me. "The Medical Examiner is doing the autopsy at ten o'clock."

"I'd like to be there."

"I was hoping you'd say that. I told Rachel about the autopsy, and she left my office without comment."

"There's a lot that comes out of an autopsy that never makes it into the final report. I like to watch the process and hear the comments. As far as I'm concerned, the medical examiner's report is little more than an abstract."

"Rachel seems a little edgy today."

"I don't think she's dealt with a dead body before, and a floater sometimes rattles even seasoned officers."

"I hope you don't feel guilty about sending her out to make the recovery."

"I was going to wade out, then she volunteered."

"Really?"

I held up three fingers. "Scout's honor."

That's not what the rumor mill says."

"The Army taught me not to believe rumors."

Matt nodded. "You were in Iraq. Were you in combat?"

"I was an M.P. assigned to base security and prison duty. I spent most of my time patrolling the housing units. Our role was supposed to be watching for terrorists, but I spent more time dealing with petty thefts and making sure the sexual encounters were consensual."

"Were a lot of women deployed?"

"The majority of the clerical personnel were women, but they were part of every non-combat unit from helicopter pilots to truck maintenance. When you throw a bunch of young men and women together, there are raging hormones and raging romances. There were too many incidents of morning-after regrets, but some incidents were outright sexual assaults. We investigated them all and took them to the adjutant general for adjudication."

"Have you ever fired your pistol off the range?"

"I have, and I can again."

"What do you mean 'can again?'"

"I knew a few cops, both in the military and the police department, who killed someone and then were so horrified by what they'd done, that they would never be able to fire their weapon in the line of duty again. They were a danger to themselves and to their partners. Most recognized that and left law enforcement."

"Do you trust Rachel to back you up if you need her?"

"It's too early to tell. I'm a little concerned about her boyfriend, Toby. He's not excited about her law enforcement career."

"How so?"

"I think he liked her being an interpretive ranger and a guide. She said he's uptight about having a gun in the house, and he makes her unload it when she comes home."

"Is that a problem?"

"Every Federal officer is expected to be prepared to use their weapon to defend themselves, their partners, or innocent civilians 24/7. If her weapon isn't loaded, she's not meeting that expectation."

"Is her gun loaded when she's on patrol?"

"I assume it is. That's part of every police training program. I haven't asked her to show me that she has a round in the chamber."

"Is there some discreet way of checking without opening a hornet's nest?"

"I really don't care if I'm opening a hornet's nest. If Rachel's not prepared to draw her weapon to protect us, I have a real problem with her."

"She could draw her weapon, work the action, then fire."

"Those extra seconds to work the action can be a life-or-death difference. The longest gunfight I've ever seen lasted ten seconds. Cops carry a round in the chamber but hold their finger alongside the trigger guard. That gives them a fraction of a second to assess the situation before their fingers are on the trigger and firing. If you need to chamber a round, that act takes your concentration away from the threat, and it adds to the time it takes to aim and fire."

Matt nodded. "You'll ask Rachel about that?"

"Yes, I will. And if she isn't prepared, I want a different partner."

"I can't get another law enforcement ranger here immediately. You'll just have to limp along with Rachel for a while if that's the case."

"No. I'll patrol alone before I go out with a partner who doesn't have my back."

I walked out the door in search of Rachel. I found her drinking coffee and chatting with two other rangers.

"Can you show me where to find a cup of coffee that's not out of a vending machine?"

"Sure," she said. I waved at the other rangers, a young man and woman who looked like they'd just graduated from college. Their uniforms were so new they still had threads sticking out of the corners of their pockets.

Rachel led me to a coffee pot in an alcove off the break area. She handed me a porcelain cup from a drying rack. "We don't use disposable cups. Wash your cup when you're through and hang it on a peg. There are containers of creamer and sugar in the cupboard.

We throw a dime into the kitty for each cup, or you can start an IOU slip in the coffee can and throw in a dollar when you get to ten cups. If you empty the carafe, the directions for making a new pot are on the back of the cupboard door."

"I take it black." I poured from the Mr. Coffee carafe, dug out a quarter, and dropped it through the slot in the lid covering the plastic can used for the kitty. "Now I'm a cup and a half ahead."

I pointed at Rachel's pistol. "How often do you requalify on the range?"

"I go to the Port Aransas PD range quarterly. Like you, I have to post my scores on-line with the Park Service. Unlike you, I'm happy to get enough shots into the center of mass on a silhouette to pass. I've never tried to make a smiley face on the silhouette."

"I was playing around. I'm happy with any partner who can put their shots into the silhouette." I took a sip of coffee and decided to go right for the question. "Is your weapon loaded?"

"What?"

"You said your boyfriend doesn't like you to have a loaded gun in the house. Is your weapon loaded now?"

"Of course, it is. I'm on duty."

"Do you have a round chambered?"

Rachel's face colored. "I'm ready to use my weapon if the situation requires me to."

147

"Is there a round in the chamber, or would you have to pull the slide to chamber a round."

"I don't see how that's any of your business."

"You're my partner. I need to know that I can rely on you if we run into a deadly encounter. I need you to have a round in the chamber, so when you draw the gun you'll be immediately prepared to fire."

"I've got your back if that's what you're asking."

"Take your weapon out of the holster and show me you've got a round in the chamber."

"Ninety-nine percent of law enforcement officers never fire their guns in the line of duty," Rachel said, with defiance.

"That's correct. But it's also true you don't need a gun until you need it badly and immediately. If I need to rely on you, I want to know you're prepared to fire your weapon as soon as it's out of your holster."

Rachel glared at me, drew her pistol, and pulled the slide back. She showed me the empty chamber and the live round on the top of the magazine. Then she released the slide, chambering a round. She slid the safety 'on' and put the Sig back in her holster. "Do you feel safer now?"

"I'm not sure. Are you willing to draw your weapon and fire it to protect my life or the life of an innocent civilian?"

"Sure."

"I'm deadly serious. If you're not prepared for that, you're in the wrong job, and you should walk away now."

"Yes, sir. I'm prepared to draw my weapon and shoot someone who's threatening your life."

"I can do without the sarcasm. Either you're ready to be a cop, or you should hand in your weapon and stand behind the counter selling brochures."

"I'm a Federal law enforcement officer. I've taken the oath. I'll do what I have to do if the need arises."

"Good," I finished my coffee and rinsed the cup. "We're going to watch an autopsy."

"Say what?"

"C'mon. The Medical Examiner is cutting at ten o'clock. We've got to get going."

"I don't think that'd be a good idea. I got sick when we pulled the body ashore and when I dissected frogs in tenth-grade biology."

"If you're a cop, you're going to see autopsies. Put on your big girl pants, and we'll be on our way."

"That's sexist."

"Are you coming, or are you staying behind to file a harassment claim and write tickets to litterers?"

"I'm coming."

Chapter 13

The drive to Corpus Christi took us over the bay. A fisherman launched a boat from a ramp on the frontage road. A bar and restaurant were on the left side of the bridge, on the right side a more upscale restaurant was located next to a bait and tackle store.

"Are either of those restaurants any good?"

"We don't eat out. Some of the rangers say the place on the left gets rowdy on the weekends. I think they like that."

"You and your boyfriend don't eat out?"

"Toby's a fulltime student. We live off my salary, and that doesn't leave a lot of money for anything but tuition, books, rent, gas, and groceries."

"I remember those days. My wife was in a Ph.D. program, and we lived off my patrolman's salary. Things were tight."

"Did your ex finish her degree?"

"She graduated while we were still married and then left for Central America to do post-doctorate work. She's an associate professor now."

"What broke up your marriage?"

"We grew apart. She started socializing with a group of grad students who didn't think much of her being married to a cop."

"Toby has a problem with that too. It's okay as long as I'm working for the Park Service, but he'd never let me take a job as a *real* cop."

"Are you planning to stay with the Park Service for the rest of your life?"

"I don't know. Matt wants to send me to the Federal law enforcement training, FLETC, if I'm going to stay on as a law enforcement ranger. I think Toby would flip out if I did that."

"You haven't told him that's the plan?"

"I think it's better to leave that topic off the table for now."

"At some point, you'll have to address it."

"We'll see what happens after Toby graduates."

"What's his major?"

"Urban studies in the sociology department. He's doing his dissertation on the effectiveness of drug rehab programs for pregnant single mothers."

"That's a pretty narrow niche."

"He thinks he can show how to reduce the number of crack-addicted babies and demonstrate how that improves the community."

"That sounds like a lifetime project. How long has Toby been in his Ph D. program?"

"Seven years so far."

"And how much longer will it take to complete it?"

"He and his advisor don't know yet. He's been following a group of women and they haven't been...they aren't as committed to rehabilitation as he thought they would be."

Once we crossed the bay, we drove through an area of shopping malls. The traffic slowed as it became more congested. I saw a sign with a blue "H" and turned off the highway. "The morgue is in the hospital."

"Yeah, I've heard that."

I glanced at Rachel. Her eyes stared straight ahead, and her right hand clenched the armrest.

"Are you okay?"

"I'm sure I'll be fine."

* * *

The gray-haired hospital receptionist wore a badge that said her name was Midge, a volunteer. "How can I help you?"

"We're going to the morgue."

Midge's cheerful expression disappeared. She pointed to her left. "Take the elevator to the basement and follow the yellow line on the floor."

The yellow line took us past the hospital laboratories, a room that said Pathology, and another that said Histology. We went through the door marked 'Morgue.' A middle-aged man wearing blue scrubs sat behind a desk filling out a form on the computer. He darkened the computer screen and turned around when he heard us enter.

"Help you?" he asked.

"We're here to watch the autopsy on the John Doe who was floating in the Gulf."

He looked at our uniforms and badges. "Park Service." He rose from the desk. "This is a first."

He led us through a pair of doors and down a short corridor, then held the door to room three for us. John Doe lay naked on a stainless-steel table like a waxy bloated mannequin. A woman, wearing scrubs, a rubber apron, gloves, a surgical mask, and a face shield examined the side of John Doe's head with gloved fingers.

"Doc," our guide said. "I've got a couple Park Service rangers here for the John Doe autopsy."

The woman looked up. "Grab a lab coat, safety goggles, and a surgical mask. I just started my external examination."

Rachel followed my lead, choosing a white, Tyvek lab coat—one size fits all—then donning a mask and goggles. We joined the doctor at the table where she examined the man's neck wound and protruding tongue. After a day of refrigeration, the body looked non-human, making this stage of the autopsy experience less gory.

The doctor didn't look up from her exam. "And you are?"

"Doug Fletcher and Rachel Randall. I'm a Park Service investigator, and Rachel is a law enforcement ranger."

The only visible parts of the doctor were her eyes and a lock of hair falling out from under her blue disposable cap. Based on the crow's feet at the corners of her eyes, I guessed she was in her fifties, but the lock of red hair made me think she might be a little younger. Fair-skinned redheads tend to get wrinkles more quickly than people with darker complexions.

"Park Service? I didn't know the Park Service had law enforcement or investigative rangers. I guess that's my lesson in humility for the day. I learn something every day. I'm Dr. Rhonda Overgaard. You may call me 'Doc.' I was just admiring the slash on this guy's throat, done in one stroke, so it must've been a very sharp knife. Used a short blade, or the attacker knew what he was doing. A deeper cut would've slashed through the lower tongue."

"The Jamaican necktie is the calling card of some gangs. I think they take great pride in doing it correctly."

The doctor looked up, appraising me. "This isn't your first rodeo."

"I've seen a few dead bodies," I replied.

"How many autopsies have you attended, Fletcher?"

"Dozens. I lost count when I got into the double digits."

"I wouldn't think the Park Service would have that many dead bodies."

154

"I was a police detective before I joined the Park Service."

"Ah," the doctor said. "How about you, Randall, have you seen many autopsies?"

"This is my first."

"There's a janitor's sink over there." The medical examiner pointed to the corner of the room. "And a bucket and mop next to the sink. If you don't make it to the sink in time, you're responsible for cleaning up your own mess."

Rachel looked stricken but nodded.

"Aside from the Jamaican necktie, and the ligatures on the wrists and ankles, the exterior of the body is unremarkable. The time he spent in the gulf washed away any evidence on the body's surface. I took fingerprints that'll be entered into the IAFIS database."

"IAFIS is the FBI database for fingerprint comparison," I explained to Rachel. "Was the neck wound the cause of death?"

"It was a post-mortem wound. It cut one carotid artery and both jugulars, but the lividity makes it clear he didn't bleed out. The marks on the left buttock look like he laid on his wallet for a while after death. He was delivered without garments. Was he naked when you recovered the body?"

"He was entirely naked when Rachel pulled him out of the surf."

The doctor looked at Rachel, who nodded.

I stepped closer and pointed to John Doe's left hand. "The broken fingernails make me think he fought with his attackers. Is there any chance we might pick up some DNA from under his nails?"

Overgaard shook her head. "I scraped them, but there wasn't anything there. The seawater did a pretty good job of removing whatever evidence I might've collected." The doctor selected a scalpel from a stainless-steel tray behind her and made an incision under the body's left armpit. "For Ranger Randall's information, I'm making a Y-incision to open the victim's chest and abdomen."

Rachel watched with apparent curiosity as the doctor made her cuts. Decomposition gasses hissed from the abdomen when the peritoneum was pierced. The nauseating stink of rotting human guts assaulted my nose. Rachel turned her head and gagged but managed to hold herself together. Next, the doctor picked up a pair of pruning shears with eighteen-inch wooden handles. "Randall, I suggest you move closer to the sink. Are you okay with this, Fletcher?"

"This is no worse than watching the PM of a gut-shot drug dealer. Right?"

Overgaard rolled her eyes, then started cutting the victim's ribs with the large shears. Rachel lasted through the crunching sounds of three ribs, then she dashed for the sink. The doctor glanced at Rachel, who was vomiting, and then looked at me, raising an eyebrow.

"I'm good," I said.

Rachel wiped her face with a paper towel and returned as the doctor examined the internal organs. "I'd say the victim was an average forty-year-old man. The liver is a little fatty, which makes me think he was probably a moderately heavy drinker. Other than that, his internal organs are unremarkable."

She took out a longer knife and sliced off a piece of the liver and held it out to her assistant. "Artie, stain a sample and look at it under the scope." Her assistant held out a stainless basin and took the liver to the counter.

Rachel grabbed my arm and held on tight. I nodded toward the sink, but she shook her head.

"His lung tissue is nice and pink, so he wasn't a smoker." The next cut was the lower lobe of the lung. Pink liquid ran into the chest cavity as she sliced. "I think we have a cause of death—John Doe drowned."

"Is that freshwater or saltwater?" I asked.

The doctor's eyes narrowed. "Did you recover the body from the ocean or a pool, Fletcher?" The doctor's voice dripped with sarcasm.

"We recovered him from the gulf, but that doesn't mean he died there."

The doctor took a specimen bottle, the kind used for a urine sample, unscrewed the cap, then ladled some water from the chest cavity into it. "Artie, take a look at this under the scope and tell me if it's seawater." Artie walked over from the bench where he'd been prepping the liver and took the specimen cup from the doctor.

She continued to take tissue samples, placing each in a specimen jar and labeling them with a Sharpie marker. She cut open the stomach and ladled some of the dark liquid into a jar.

"His last meal has already passed through his stomach. This looks and smells like smoked almonds. Maybe his last stop was a bar."

"Smoked almonds aren't normal bar food," I said. "It'd have to be someplace pretty upscale, or he just got off a plane and was sitting in first class."

The doctor screwed the cap on the jar and marked it with a Sharpie. "Listen, Fletcher, I'm not used to having a cop second guess everything I say."

"Hey, I'm not arguing with you. I'm just not satisfied with the first answer that comes to mind."

"I've found the first thing that comes to mind is the correct answer about ninety-nine percent of the time," the doctor responded.

"Doc," Artie said. "The sample you gave me is freshwater. There are no plankton or other signs of an oceanic source."

The surgical mask hid my smile, but not the twinkle in my eye. "Okay, Fletcher, so you were right once. But don't let it go to your head. And you *could* be right about the smoked almonds. They would be consistent with someone riding in first class."

"How long has he been dead?" I asked.

"It's hard to pinpoint." The doctor continued to inspect the heart and other internal organs. "It's been at least eighteen hours, because all rigor is gone from the muscles, and there's been enough internal decomposition to cause his belly to inflate. I'd say he's been in the water less than twenty-four hours."

"You didn't find any distinguishing marks on the body or anything that might help us identify him?"

"He didn't have a tattoo, birthmark, watch, ring, or a scar. No pacemaker or surgical implants. He's never had a broken bone. There's nothing to help us identify him."

"Is there anything else for us to hang around for?"

"We'll do a tox screen on his blood, but we know he drowned. I can't think of any reason you need to hang around."

"Thanks, Doc." We turned to leave and started stripping off our gowns.

"Hey, Fletcher." I turned around. "That was a good catch on the water in the lungs. I would've blown past that if you hadn't asked."

The lab assistant looked up from a machine on the counter. "I checked the chlorine. It was tap water, not pool water. The chlorine levels were much lower than pool or hot tub water, and there is a trace of fluoride in it."

The doctor nodded, apparently acknowledging my observations. "Good luck, guys. Your work is cut out for you."

"Thanks, Doc."

* * *

We were back on the highway before Rachel spoke. "I'm sorry. I hoped I'd be able to keep it together, but when she started cutting the guy's ribs, I just lost it."

"You did well. Most people are vomiting when the gas escapes from the abdomen. I've seen cops pass out during the rib cutting." I paused, but Rachel seemed unconvinced. "I had a partner who wouldn't go to an autopsy. He just told the coroner to send him the report."

"The doctor seemed pretty impressed that you asked about freshwater versus seawater. What made you even think of that."

"It was a hunch."

"The doctor said our job was cut out for us. What did she mean?"

"The coroner is usually able to identify the victim, and most murders are committed by someone known to the victim. The significant other is usually our first interview, and I've often gotten either a remorseful confession or a solid lead from that first interview."

"So, we don't know who the significant other is. Where do we start?"

"Your next job is calling the Coast Guard to see which direction the current flows along the shore, and how fast it moves. I assume he must've washed down from Mustang Island because there's no way a north-flowing current would've carried him all the way here from the nearest access on South Padre Island in eighteen hours."

"What are you going to do?"

"I'm calling the airlines flying into Corpus Christi to see who was in first-class about twenty-four hours ago. Then, we start calling hotels to see if they're missing any guests."

"But that'll take hundreds of calls."

I smiled. "Police work isn't just ticketing speeders and yelling at litterers. It's boring, and usually fruitless, phone calls and shoe leather."

Chapter 14

I briefed Matt on the autopsy, then went to the empty office I'd adopted as my own and started calling. Only two airlines fly into Corpus Christi, and it took a few phone calls to find someone who could, and would, give me the manifests of first-class customers. They all confirmed that the flight crews were based out of Dallas, but no way would I get their names much less phone numbers. So, I couldn't ask the cabin attendants if they recalled a customer eating smoked almonds.

Most of the first-class passengers were men, so that didn't narrow the list of potential victims, but one of the American Airlines people threw me a clue. If the passenger hadn't had a meal recently, his flight either originated in Dallas, or he'd probably flown in on a red-eye flight that didn't have meal service. She threw me another bone, too. Only three passengers had flown one-way or with open return tickets.

Rachel was back with a map in half an hour. "Toby called and said he's got chili cooking. Are you and Jill free tonight?"

"I don't know." I pulled out my cellphone and dialed Jill. "We've got a dinner invitation. Do you have plans for tonight?"

"I bought pork chops, but I can put them in the refrigerator."

"Jill says we're free."

"Come over about six." She took the piece of paper I'd been writing on, scribbled an address on the corner and tore it off. "Here's our address."

"We've got a dinner invitation for six," I relayed to Jill.

"What's the dress code?"

"Jill wants to know what to wear."

I hit speakerphone so Rachel could talk to Jill without my mediation. "It's college student casual."

"Got it! Shorts and sandals."

I disconnected the call and helped Rachel unroll the map she set on my desktop. "What's this?"

"I've got Coast Guard current and wind information." We set a coffee cup, a stapler, the phone, and an empty picture frame leftover from the previous occupant on the four map corners. "They said the current isn't very strong, and the body was most likely moved by the wind pushing the waves south. Here's where we recovered the body." She'd put a red "X" on that location.

Then she put a ruler on the shore and started putting black dashes on the map. "So, the estimates for wind drift are rough, but each of these represents about two hours of drift given the weather pattern for the last two days." She quit when she had sixteen marks on the map, representing thirty-two hours of drift.

"This mark is between the county park and the first condo building. If John Doe has been in the water less than twenty hours, he would've been dumped somewhere inside the Park Service boundary, or no further north than the Mustang Beach rental kiosk, here. The beach rental place is right where 361 turns toward Corpus Christi and becomes Highway 358. There's a fishing pier here, at the county park by Packery Channel. The park is deserted after dark, so that'd be a perfect place to drop a body into the water. That's about where I'd estimate a body would've started before fourteen hours of drifting and if they dropped it as the tide was going out, it'd be pulled right offshore."

"That shoots my theory of someone killing him and dragging his body to the beach outside a Mustang Island hotel," I said.

"Well, it does put him in the area and within a short drive of anything on Mustang Island. It also puts him at the pier in the dark. If I were dumping a body, I'd do it in the dark when there's no one around."

"I've got three possible travelers who flew in first class in the right timeframe." I pushed the phonebook to her. "Rip out the motels' section and start calling. See if any of these three people checked in and ask whether they're still there or not."

Rachel gave me "the look" and pushed the phonebook back to me. "I'll look them up on my cellphone and call directly from the internet listings. What are you going to do?"

"I'll call the condos, asking the same question."

"If I don't get a hit before quitting time, I'll see you at six," Rachel said and left.

I shook my head. Being a cop wasn't a nine-to-five job. Rachel had a lot to learn if she was going to be a successful cop.

* * *

I left the admin building about five-thirty and drove to the townhouse. Jill met me at the door holding a pink golf shirt and a pair of khaki shorts. "Mandy and I found a sale and bought something for you to wear tonight. Change quickly, you're running late."

I held up the shirt. "Pink? Really?"

"It'll put some color into your pasty complexion. Take a quick shower and put these on. I'm ready to go."

I rushed the shower. The pink shirt didn't fit my sense of style, but I decided against irritating Jill by looking for an alternative. I padded out in my bare feet, clipping the Sig holster to my belt and pulling the shirttail over the gun. It stood out like a gun does under any t-shirt. Jill handed me another new pair of sandals. "I looked in your shoes, and these are your size."

"I have tennis shoes."

"No, you don't. You threw them away after wading in the toxic muck. Besides, you have to get into Texas-style." She watched as I adjusted the straps.

"I thought Texas-style was jeans and cowboy boots?"

She tossed me the keys, and I locked the door as I went through. I handed Jill the address torn from the corner of my notepad. "Here's the address. Punch it into your phone and find a route."

"Turn on 361."

"I didn't even look at the address. Where are we going?"

She studied the smartphone screen. "We're going someplace in Corpus Christi, not far from the bay."

"How was your day?"

"Mandy called as I stepped out of the shower and asked if I had lunch plans. After lunch at a little café, we found a tourist shop that's going out of business, and I bought those clothes for you. After she dropped me off, I made a couple more fruitless marina calls, then went to the gym for an hour. It was a nice day. How about you?"

"Rachel and I went to the John Doe autopsy."

"And…" Jill waited for me to expand on my comments.

"He had no identifying marks, no tattoos, and no scars."

"No way to identify him?"

"The M.E. will check his fingerprints. If she can find a probable identification, she'll have to match dental records. Until then, all we've got to go on is that he'd been eating smoked almonds, and we know he probably drowned in a bathtub."

"But his throat was slit, and you found him in the ocean. He didn't drown there?"

"Apparently not. Someone drowned him, slit his throat, then dumped his body into the gulf."

"If he drowned in a pool at a motel or condo, you'd think someone would've noticed."

"The chemicals in the water makes it more likely he died in tap water, like a bathtub."

"Oh, turn at this next exit, then take a left on the cross street going under the highway." Once I made the turns, Jill asked, "How are you going to identify him and track down his killers?

"The medical examiner is running his fingerprints. I checked with the airlines, and there are a limited number of people who were seated in first class where you get smoked almonds. I've got three people who either flew one-way or had open returns. We're going to focus on them and see if any of them are missing from their hotel or condo."

Jill looked around as I drove slowly through the residential streets. "This neighborhood is old. The yards are small, and quite a few houses have bikes or toys in the yard." She pointed at a house ahead of us. "I think it's the green house on the right."

I parked and tucked the Sig under the seat before locking the doors. Rachel met us at the front door wearing a tie-dyed dress made of t-shirt material and belted with a white rope. Her hair was tied in a short ponytail. The house was warm and filled with the aroma of onions and peppers.

"Hi Rachel. This is my friend, Jill."

She hugged us. "I'm so glad you guys could come on short notice. Toby, come out here and meet Doug and Jill."

Toby appeared from the kitchen, wiping his hands on his cut-off jeans. He was shirtless, his chest covered with a thick mat of dark hair that matched his mustache and beard. He wore a headband made from a red bandana holding back his long hair.

"Hey," he said with a Texas twang. He shook my hand. "You're the cop, right?" He hugged Jill, who wasn't a hugging person. It looked like she squirmed herself out of his arms before he let go.

"I'm a Park Service investigator. I was a city cop in a previous life."

"An investigator isn't a cop?"

"Not really. I don't hand out speeding tickets or look for people with outstanding arrest warrants."

"But you carry a gun and arrest people."

"I haven't fired my weapon or arrested anyone in a while."

He looked at Rachel. "Maybe you should be an investigator. You wouldn't have to go around harassing speeders and people who are littering." He wasn't smiling.

Rachel turned red. "Is the chili ready?"

A kitchen timer dinged as if on cue, and Toby turned away. "I'll pull the cornbread out of the oven."

I looked around the living room at the garage sale chairs and sagging sofa. An old CRT television sat on top of four cement blocks. What looked like a pirated cable box was wired to the television, reminding me of my days as a college student. Their coffee table was a plank set on top of two cement blocks. A lamp with a tattered shade sat on an old fruit crate.

"I smell the cornbread," Jill said, sniffing the air.

Rachel directed us to the tiny kitchen. "Come, sit at the table."

We sat on mismatched folding chairs. Rachel seated me in the one wooden chair. Two ceramic tiles had been set on the chipped Formica table as trivets. Toby set a square baking tin of browned cornbread on one trivet. Rachel set a cast iron pot containing a gallon of chili on the other.

"I heard you guys were from up north," Toby said, ladling chili into his own bowl. He handed the ladle to me. "I hope I didn't make this too hot for y'all."

Rachel cut the cornbread into squares and put the first one on Jill's plate. Toby dug his fork into one and crumbled it onto his chili. I took the next square, and Rachel took one for herself.

Rachel stood abruptly. "Oh, goodness, where are my manners. Would you like iced tea or a glass of water?"

We accepted tea. Toby had brought his own glass of tea to the table but didn't offer any to us. I was unsure if it was a slight or just poor manners. I heard ice cubes fall into glasses, and then the sound of tea being poured from a pitcher.

I tasted the chili and knew I was in trouble. I'd had spicy food before, but this was hotter than anything I'd ever eaten. I could see Jill reacting to the spice, too. She took a tissue out of her pocket and wiped her nose.

Toby noted Jill's reaction. "I toned the chili down a bit. I call this three-alarm chili. I make four-alarm chili when it's just Rachel and me eating."

I felt perspiration beading on my forehead. Rachel handed me a frosty glass of iced tea. I knew it wouldn't put out the burn, but I had to get something cool into my mouth. She'd made Southern-style sweet tea—so sweet it almost made my teeth ache.

Rachel read my thoughts. "If the chili's too hot, crumble some cornbread into it."

"I usually put a dab of sour cream in my chili," I said.

Toby shook his head. "We're vegan. We don't use any animal products."

I nodded and crumbled cornbread on the chili. It diluted the heat but didn't kill the burn. I hoped my taste buds would be overwhelmed at some point and stop sending pain messages to my brain.

Jill set her spoon aside and drizzled honey from an earthenware bowl on her cornbread. "You're vegan, but you wear leather boots."

Toby shook his head. "That's different. The cow was dead."

Jill nodded, but I could see that logic didn't sell her on the response.

"So, what's in your chili?" I was working on my fourth spoonful of chili, hoping I'd be able to make it through the whole bowl like my mother always told me polite guests did. The heat didn't seem to be affecting Toby or Rachel.

Toby scooped up another bowlful of chili for himself. "There's jalapenos, kidney beans, tomatoes, cilantro, cumin, chili powder, red peppers, and tofu."

I pushed a spongy, dark mass around the bowl, guessing it was tofu. I'm not a big tofu fan, but I hoped it might put out some of the burn in my mouth. It seemed like the tofu had absorbed a disproportionate share of the spice. I swallowed it without chewing and took a big drink of tea. I looked at Jill, who smiled, enjoying my attempt at being a good guest. She had pushed her chili aside and was drizzling honey on a second piece of cornbread.

Rachel finished her chili and pushed the bowl aside. "What do you do, Jill?"

"I'm on leave from the Park Service. I work in Flagstaff."

"That's where you met Doug?" Rachel asked.

I'd paused halfway through my chili. "Yes."

"We were co-workers," Jill interjected before I had a chance to expand on my answer.

Toby was suddenly interested in the conversation. "Is your relationship with Doug why you're on leave? Is fraternization a big no-no in the Park Service?"

"Doug and I didn't start dating until after I started my leave." Jill licked the honey from her fingers. "This is really great cornbread, Toby. I wouldn't know how to make it without using an egg. What's your recipe?"

"Cornmeal, flour, water, baking soda, baking powder, corn oil, and some maple syrup."

"Ah, it's the maple flavor that had me stumped. It's really good. I'd like the recipe."

Toby seemed pleased. "I'll write it down for you after supper."

Jill pushed her plate aside. "How long have you two been together?"

Rachel jumped in before Toby had a chance to answer. "We met as undergrads. I guess it's been like eight years now."

Toby nodded. "The quality of our mutual beliefs makes our bond strong."

"Have you ever considered marriage?"

Rachel froze and looked at Toby, who replied, "Marriage is an artificial church-run scam to promote monogamy. Humans never evolved to be monogamous."

Jill cocked her head. "You have an open relationship?"

Toby scraped the last of the chili from his bowl. "We're together, but we keep our options open."

"Doug has an ex-wife who felt the same way." I almost choked on my chili and gave Jill a look like she'd strayed into forbidden territory, but my mouth was full and on fire, so I couldn't respond.

Toby jumped on her response. "That's a perfect example. You get tangled up in a marriage, and sometimes one person grows away. Then you have to go through the system to get uncoupled."

I wiped my mouth with a paper towel. "She was sleeping with some of the other students."

Toby gave me a *so-what* shrug.

Rachel got up and gathered bowls. "I made some orange sorbet."

Toby smiled. "Are you trying to change the subject?"

"Yes."

We ate the sorbet without further relationship discussions. Jill was able to connect with Toby by talking about her efforts to preserve ruins in Flagstaff, and then we bid an early farewell after Rachel refused our offer to help wash dishes.

I took a deep breath and sighed, then started the Isuzu. "Is this what you had in mind when you said you wanted to socialize?"

Jill was reveling in my discomfort. "Is your tongue bleeding from biting it?"

"My tongue's on fire, and my blood pressure is probably off-scale from choking back all the things I'd like to have said."

Jill patted my arm. "Now, now. They're young and in love. At some point, they'll get a clue."

"I doubt Toby will ever get a clue. By the time you're deep into a doctoral program, your views are pretty well entrenched."

"I think he lives in rarified university air where you're above the average person's ability to understand the true solutions that would make this world right if only they'd listen to him."

I pulled away from the curb and made an illegal U-turn. "He's in that same environment as my ex-wife. Everything is black and white."

Jill pointed to the right as I approached the highway overpass. "Turn onto the frontage road."

"Why?" I barely made the corner.

"I'm hungry, and I saw an interesting bar-b-que place when we went by earlier."

'Rudy's' flashed in red neon over a red barn-like structure on the frontage road. I pulled into a surprisingly busy parking lot considering the late hour. Jill was out of the Isuzu before it stopped rolling. We studied the menu posted behind the cash register while standing in a line behind a dozen people. Most of the choices were different cuts of meat, available in quarter-pound increments. We passed a bin filled with ice-covered soda pop, and a refrigerator full of plastic coleslaw and potato salad containers. When we got to the counter, a well-fed guy in a red apron leaned toward us. "Whatcha want?"

I pointed at the overhead menu. "I'm a little lost. I see meat by the pound. Do we get sandwiches or meals, or what?"

"You never been to Rudy's before. You order your meat, pick a side if you want it, and grab a drink from the cooler or order a tap beer here. You pick up your meat at the end and take it to the other room. There's bread there if you want to eat your meat that way."

I scanned the menu again. "Which are beef and which are pork?"

"Sir, this is Texas. It's beef. If you want pork, you gotta go to someplace where they raise pigs." The word "pigs" was spat out with obvious disdain.

"Give us a half-pound of brisket," Jill said. She was smiling because I'd asked the question on her mind and gotten the reprimand.

The guy punched our order into the register. "You want wet or dry?"

I searched the menu for a hint. "What's the difference?"

The guys eyes narrowed like I was stupid. "The dry is drier, and the wet is wetter."

"We want wet," Jill's quick response garnered a smile.

"You having a soda, beer, or just the meat?"

I was about to ask about the beer options when the guy anticipated my question and pointed to the Lone Star tap behind him. I nodded and gave him a thumbs up.

"You two look like you might be over twenty-one." He told us the price, then turned to tap our beers.

I reached for my wallet, but Jill pulled a debit card out of her back pocket. "I've got it."

When he returned with the beer, I asked, "Do you take debit cards?"

The man snatched the debit card from Jill's hand and put it into a slot on the cash register. "You may be south of the Mason Dixon line, sir, but you're not on the moon." He handed the card and a cash register slip to Jill. "Your meat will be down there," he said, pointing down the stainless-steel counter.

"Thank you," Jill said, sparkling.

"What's a cute bright girl like you doing with a guy who doesn't even know about Texas bar-b-que?"

Jill grinned. "It's a blind date."

The man nodded knowingly.

We watched the other customers and followed the protocol of taking bread out of bags on a counter. We spread butcher paper on the table for use as a tablecloth/plate and used plastic utensils to pull strips of meat off the brisket slices. Jill speared a small piece of meat and popped it in her mouth while I squeezed sauce over the sandwich I'd assembled.

Jill's eyes went wide. "Oh, my. I think I've died and gone to heaven."

I took a bite. "Wow!"

Jill ate brisket directly from the basket without the bread. "Pretty good for a shot in the dark." She sipped her beer.

I must've looked angry.

"Ease up, Fletcher."

"Why did you bring up my ex-wife?"

"I thought it would help you connect with Toby."

"You waited until I had a mouthful of chili and then threw it out like a hand grenade when I couldn't defend myself."

She patted my arm. "You're overreacting. Besides, it moved us on to a different topic."

"It let you slip your chili aside and move to cornbread and honey."

Jill waited a few bites before moving the conversation to a new topic. "I think the guy at the counter was hitting on me."

"You're old enough to be…"

"Careful, Fletcher. You're on thin ice."

I studied her smile for a second. "You have a pretty smile."

"Nice recovery." She set down her fork and squeezed my hand.

Seeing her dimples made me smile. "You had a good time tonight."

"I like getting out and socializing. I haven't been to anyone's house in ages."

"I didn't enjoy it as much as you did."

"Rachel was delightful. She was trying so hard to be a good hostess." She waited a beat, then added, "Toby's hair smelled like marijuana smoke."

"When did you sniff his hair?"

"When he gave me the overly long hug and tried to slide his hand onto my butt."

"I didn't notice that."

"You were getting your own uncomfortable hug from Rachel."

"He put his hand on your butt?"

"He was moving that direction. Just before he got to my belt, I whispered he'd lose his hand if it went any lower. Our hug ended pretty quickly after that." She got up and walked to the stainless-steel sink built into the side of the room and washed her hands while I finished the last pieces of brisket. The guy who took our order came into the dining room and wiped tables. When Jill passed, he said something to her, and she laughed, then patted him on the arm.

I finished my beer, dumped our tray into the garbage, and met her at the door.

"What did he say that made you laugh?"

"He told me every couple has a fun person and a fun sponge who can suck the fun out of any situation. He said I was obviously the fun one, and you are the sponge."

I unlocked and opened the vehicle door for her.

She pecked me on the cheek. "It's funny after me being the fun sponge for decades."

Chapter 15

Friday Morning

I showered, trying not to wake Jill but failed. I smelled coffee when I toweled off. Since I planned to sit in the office all day making phone calls, I opted for a western-cut short sleeve shirt and khaki pants rather than my uniform. I pinned the Park Service badge to the shirt, but it seemed out of place, so I put it back into my wallet.

Jill had a cup of coffee waiting for me when I walked into the kitchen. She was wrapped in a terrycloth robe I didn't recognize as anything that had been unpacked from the tiny bag she'd brought to San Antonio. For that matter, most of her Port Aransas wardrobe had been acquired while shopping with Mandy Mattson and it had filled her drawers and more than half the closet. I took that as I sign that she might be putting down roots.

She was buttering toast. "Do you want these pieces of toast, or would you rather have cereal?"

"Toast would be great, but I can make my own."

She waved off my offer, set the plate in front of me, and stuck two more pieces of bread into the toaster for herself.

I pulled a jar of peanut butter out of the cupboard and grabbed a knife from the silverware drawer.

"Would you grab the prickly pear jam?" she asked as I passed the refrigerator.

I grabbed the pink jar, set it on the table next to her coffee cup, and then spread Jif on my toast. "I can't say I'm a fan of the pink jam."

"It's got an interesting flavor, and it's not as overwhelmingly sweet as most commercial jam."

"Where are you at with your calls to the marinas?"

"I've called nineteen, and none of them had an owner with a blue bass boat, nor had anyone launched a blue bass boat recently. I think our hazardous waste dumper has his boat moored or tied up to a private pier somewhere. I've got a couple more calls to make, but I'm running out of marinas." Jill sighed. "What's your plan for today?"

"I've got three names. They're people who flew in first-class during the right time period. Rachel and I have split up the list of hotels and condos hoping to find these men, and with luck, one of them is our John Doe."

"And if you don't identify John Doe that way, what's your plan?"

"I don't have a plan B, yet."

"It seems unlikely you'd stumble across the right person based on your guess."

"It's all I've got right now. What's your plan after you call the last marinas?"

"I'm going to the gym, then I thought I'd take a long walk around the residential area west of the highway. There are still a lot of houses that haven't been repaired since the hurricane, and it makes me wonder what's going on. I like to speculate on who owns them, and why they haven't been repaired yet."

"It's been tough. The price of construction materials has skyrocketed, and there aren't enough construction people to do all the jobs that are available. I imagine some of those houses will be bulldozed, and the lots put up for sale."

"It seems sad. It's such a pretty area with boat access to the gulf."

Jill cleared the table while I poured coffee into a thermal mug.

She kissed me at the door. "Good luck with your John Doe."

* * *

I was on my fourth condo call when Rachel stuck her head in the door.

"You're already hard at it." She pulled a guest chair next to the desk and sat down. "It was fun to have you guys over."

"Toby doesn't like cops, and that's certainly his prerogative, but it must strain your relationship."

"We work around it," Rachel said with a shrug. "It seemed like the three-alarm chili was a little too hot for Jill's taste."

"It had some bite, but I got through mine."

"Jill was really nice. I think you're a lucky guy."

"I think I'm lucky, too."

"So, we're back to calling hotels and condos again, or are we driving the beach?"

"I'm digging into the condo list. I think checking the hotels for these guys is a higher priority than driving the empty beach."

"I'll call hotels this morning, and we'll drive the beach this afternoon. How's that sound?"

"A decision worthy of Solomon," I replied.

The condo calls were getting me nowhere. I walked to the coffee pot and poured myself a cup. One of the younger rangers came in and added to his IOU slip before pouring himself a coffee.

"I'm Kevin," he said, reaching out his hand. "I heard you're the new law enforcement ranger." He appraised my casual attire but said nothing.

"Doug Fletcher," I said, shaking his hand.

"I heard you made Rachel wade out and drag in a dead body."

"Is that what she's telling people?"

"She's making herself sound like a real martyr, doing all the work while you leaned against the fender and watched."

"There was no point in both of us getting wet."

Kevin laughed. "This is the biggest thing that's happened in her entire ranger career. Having her wade out was the best thing you could've done for her self-esteem. She's a different person."

"Thanks for the perspective."

"By the way, coffee costs a dime."

"I put in a quarter yesterday."

"Sure, you did." Kevin smiled as he walked out the door.

I dug a nickel out of my pocket and threw it into the plastic container hard enough to be heard in the hallway.

Rachel nearly bowled me over as I came out of the coffee cubby hole. She had a laptop computer under her arm. "Doug, you weren't in your office. I found one of the guys. He's staying at the Holiday Inn, and I talked to him. He's just fine."

"Good job! Now we're down to two."

"No," she shook her head. "I finished the hotels and decided to do an internet search on the other two guys. One lives in Corpus Christi, so he isn't staying on the island. I called his house and talked to one of his kids. He's at his office. The other guy is from Minnesota. I called his house and got an answering machine, so I left a message."

We walked to my office, and Rachel closed the door. "I also did an internet search to find out more about the Minnesota guy."

"Who does he work for? They might be able to tell us why he's in Texas."

It took a few minutes for Rachel's computer to boot up, but once it connected to the wi-fi, her fingers flew over the keys.

"He's an assistant county attorney for Hennepin County."

"Minneapolis is the county seat. Can you get a phone number for the office?"

She spun the computer around and pointed to the phone number.

I dialed, and a receptionist answered on the second ring. "This is Douglas Fletcher, I'm with the U.S. Park Service. I'm trying to locate Ted Kaplan. Can you connect me with his office?"

"Please hold." I was left listening to a piano version of Barry Manilow's "Copa Cabana."

"Ranger Fletcher?" a deep male voice asked.

"Yes, is this Ted Kaplan?"

"My name is Roger Parker. I'm the county attorney. May I ask about your interest in Ted Kaplan?"

"I'm actually a Park Service Investigator with a case in Texas. Ted Kaplan fits the profile of a John Doe we've recovered."

"Where are you, Fletcher?"

"Padre Island National Seashore, across the bay from Corpus Christi."

"Please give me your number. I'll have someone get back to you."

"Do you know where Ted Kaplan is?"

"Fletcher, I'm not at liberty to say anything more to a stranger on the phone. Give me a number where you can be reached while I verify your identity."

"Matt Mattson is the park superintendent and my supervisor." Rachel scribbled a number on a piece of paper and slid it over to me. "Here's the park's main number."

"What did you learn from that?" Rachel asked as I hung up the phone.

"I think Ted Kaplan is missing, and Roger Parker didn't want to share that information with someone cold-calling him. You may have found the needle in the haystack."

I heard a door creak down the hallway. "Fletcher!" Matt yelled.

"Come on, Rachel."

Matt sat at his desk with his hand over the phone. "I've got the Hennepin County Attorney on the phone. Let me put him on the speaker."

"Mr. Parker, I have Investigator Fletcher and Ranger Rachel Randall with me."

"Thanks for verifying Fletcher's credentials. I've got several pieces of information you need. Ted Kaplan didn't show up for a court appearance this past Monday. We searched for him and had the local police do a wellness check on his home. He wasn't there, and they didn't find any evidence of foul play, nor did they find any indication of where he might've gone. They were unable to locate Ted's laptop computer or his briefcase with his files and notes.

"Ted's one of our senior prosecutors, and he always stays in touch with the office. His disappearance is totally out of character. What makes you think he may be a John Doe in Texas?"

"Ranger Randall and I recovered a body from the Gulf Monday afternoon. The person had been murdered and set into the water naked, without identification. Based on the autopsy, we looked at people who'd flown into Corpus Christi in the twenty-four hours before the murder, and we have been trying to track down the men on that list."

"What makes you think Ted might've flown to Corpus Christi?"

"He flew in on a redeye flight after connecting through Dallas."

"Do you have any idea why?" Parker asked.

"We were hoping you'd be able to answer that question."

"I have no idea. He was preparing the opening arguments in a major case scheduled for Monday morning. All hell broke loose when he didn't show up in the courtroom. Luckily, one of our junior people was there to ask for a continuance while we looked for Ted, but the judge was not pleased, nor has her disposition improved in the days since then while we've been trying to patch his case together from our office notes and his emails."

Rachel tapped her ring finger.

"Is Mr. Kaplan married?"

"It's interesting you should ask. His wife is missing too."

"Please describe Mr. Kaplan."

"He was average height, with medium length brown hair. I'm afraid he was physically unremarkable. I don't recall anything that would help identify his body, like a scar or tattoo."

"Can you locate his dental records?"

"Offhand, I don't know who his dentist was, but I can ask my assistant to talk to the local police. Perhaps they can find a dentist bill or a business card."

"He probably has the number on his cellphone and computer," I suggested.

"They're both missing. Not having Ted's computer is one of the things making it so difficult to reconstruct his case."

"How thoroughly did you search his house?"

"The local police broke into the house and verified that neither Ted nor his wife was there. We were initially concerned there had been a crime, but once the police determined they were not there and the house didn't look like a crime scene, they checked for Ted's laptop computer and phone, then they sealed the house and left."

"I assume you've contacted his parents and in-laws."

"Yes. We contacted them all on Monday. They haven't seen or heard from Ted or Wendy since before his disappearance. We've also contacted brothers and sisters, and they haven't heard from either of them. It's all very mysterious."

"We'll have the medical examiner contact your office, and they can work on locating dental records. I hope we don't need to approach the parents or siblings for DNA samples for the identification."

"Can you email John Doe's picture to us? Perhaps we can confirm the identity from a picture."

"What's your email address? We can send a picture, but the body had been in the water for about a day and, well, he might not...look the same."

He gave me his email address, then added, "We deal with crime scene photos all the time. I think we can handle it."

I looked at Rachel, who was busy on her computer. "It's on the way."

We heard a keyboard clicking. "It's already here." There was a pause, then a sigh. "I'm ninety-nine percent sure that's Ted. I'll contact his parents."

Matt leaned close to the speaker. "Can you guess why he'd be here?"

"I have no idea why he'd fly to Texas on the eve of a huge case."

"Are his parents here, or did he ever vacation here?" Rachel asked.

"His parents live locally, and his siblings are mostly in this area. His in-laws live in

Central Wisconsin. I have no idea where he spent his vacations."

"Does he have an administrative assistant who might know?"

"Hang on," Parker obviously wanted to move on from our conversation. We listened to music for another minute.

"Hello, this is Janet Levi, Mr. Kaplan's assistant. How can I help you?"

"Have you spoken with Mr. Parker?" I asked.

"No, he just asked me to pick up the line."

"This is Doug Fletcher, an investigator with the Park Service in Padre Island National Seashore. I'm here with Park Superintendent Mattson and Ranger Randall. We recovered a body we believe is Mr. Kaplan."

We heard a gasp. "Really? Are you sure?"

"Mr. Parker looked at a picture of the victim, and he identified the body as Mr. Kaplan. I'm sorry you heard about this over the phone. I assume you and Mr. Kaplan were close."

"I've been his admin assistant for eight years. We knew each other well. Has anyone notified Wendy?"

"Wendy is Mr. Kaplan's wife?"

"Yes. She'll be devastated."

"Have you spoken with Mrs. Kaplan?"

"Mr. Parker had me try to call her, but she hasn't been answering her home or cellphone. I had the local police do a wellness check on

Kaplan's, but there's no one at the house and no sign of a crime."

"Can you think of any reason Mr. Kaplan would've come to Texas, Ms. Levi?"

"He was preparing for a big trial that started Monday. There's no way he would've gone out of town right now."

"Did he have any connections in Texas. Maybe a former business partner, a college roommate, or a relative?"

There was a pause. "He and Wendy have a condo on a beach. I can't remember the name of the island, but it's on the Gulf of Mexico."

"Mustang Island?"

"That sounds right. Is that somewhere near you?"

"It's just down the road. Do you know the name of the condo building?"

"I'm sure he mentioned it, but I can't recall the name."

"Thank you." Matt reached to turn off the speakerphone when Ms. Levi spoke.

"What's happening with Mr. Kaplan's body?"

"He's in the morgue in Corpus Christi."

"I'll talk to his parents and see what they'd like to do. I can help them with the arrangements."

"Thank you, Ms. Levi."

Chapter 16

Matt disconnected the call and smiled. "Good work, guys. That was awesome."

I nodded to my partner. "Rachel did a nice job of putting the pieces together and using the internet to search for the last three guys." She beamed.

"What's next?" Matt asked.

"We need to find Kaplan's condo. His wife is missing too. Maybe she's at the condo and will answer the door."

"If she's not?" Matt asked.

"We'll request the local police make a wellness check on Kaplan's wife. If she doesn't answer, they'll have to get a search warrant."

"What would you expect to find?"

"A bloody bathtub, a knife, some ligatures, Kaplan's clothes, and a cellphone."

"Maybe the missing computer," Rachel added.

Matt leaned back and looked conflicted. "Do we need to call the FBI? I think the protocol is to consult them in any major crimes on Park Service property."

"There's been no crime here. We found a body, and he was probably murdered someplace up on Mustang Island. All we're doing is aiding the local police with an investigation."

Matt frowned. "I take it you don't like the idea of involving the FBI, Doug."

"I haven't gotten any warm fuzzies from dealing with them. And, I don't see a role for them in this investigation."

"It looks like there's an interstate aspect to it."

"If the local police want to call them in, I won't interfere, but I'm not interested in inviting them in based on what I've seen so far."

Matt leaned back. "I'll let you make the call."

Rachel was at my side as we walked back to my office. "Are we going to call the condos or are you going to leave that to the Port Aransas cops?"

"Let's make the calls. It might be too early to call in the locals, and I don't want to cry wolf."

We sat in my office, and I pulled out the phone book and opened it to the yellow pages. "Rachel, you take A through M. I'll take N through Z."

"You know half of the names in the phone book start with Aransas, Corpus, or Mustang, so I'll end up with three-quarters of the calls." She had a sheepish grin.

I put on my best surprised look. "Really?"

Rachel pulled her cellphone out of her pocket. "I'll call the county property tax office to see if they can locate a deed for Ted Kaplan.

You start with the Zs and see how far you can work backward before I have the answer."

She flipped through the pages to the condo section and went to the end, then spun the book toward me. The last listing was Thomas Village. "Oh, look at the progress you've made. You've already gone through everything from Z through T, and after the one T listing, there's nothing until R. You are so efficient."

"Call the county. I'm getting some warm coffee."

I hung up on my fifth fruitless call when Rachel walked in beaming.

"Guess what? All the county property records are computerized, and it took them about two minutes to find a property with Theodore and Wendy Kaplan listed as the owners."

I feigned amazement. "It took that long."

"The only reason it took that long is I had them start with Ted Kaplan before we theorized Ted was a nickname. Theodore Kaplan popped right up." Rachel handed me a computer printout of the property record for Aransas Wharf Condominiums.

I visualized the sign at the condo entrance. "I pass this place every morning and night."

"We lucked out." Rachel sat in my guest chair. "The county recorder pointed out we may have found the body on the Padre Island, but he could've been murdered anywhere and dumped here."

"Rookie mistake on my part," I said. "But, if I could only search by calling all these condos, I'd still have started on Mustang Island, and then worked my way up to Rockford and across the bay to Corpus Christi."

"Lucky you have me, the technology expert," Rachel said, smiling.

"Expertise is relative."

"True. Relative to you, I'm a technology guru."

"Grab your Smokey Bear hat. We're going to knock on the door at Kaplan's condo."

"Are you sure this is a good idea? What if the killers are still there?"

We walked to the Park Service pickup. "We're not going to actually knock on the door. I'm planning to find a superintendent or manager. I hope they'll be aware of who's been coming and going from the condo. Then, we'll talk to a few of the neighbors."

"You told Matt the local cops will need a search warrant to get into the apartment."

"Not if we can find Wendy Kaplan and get permission to look around."

"That's an interesting point—where is Wendy Kaplan if she's not in the condo? Do you think she's the murderer?"

"A Jamaican necktie isn't a woman's calling card. Whoever cut Kaplan's throat did it in one swipe with a very sharp knife. To do that, the killer had to have overpowered and drowned Kaplan, and I don't see his wife having the strength or the stomach to do something like that."

"So, how do women kill people?" Rachel asked as we exited the National Seashore and got on Highway 361.

"Traditionally, poison has been a woman's murder weapon. As society has become more violent, we were seeing more female stabbers and shooters."

"This wasn't a stabbing, shooting, or poison."

"No, this was a drowning, and it's unlikely Wendy Kaplan tied up her husband and drowned him."

"She could've hired someone to kill him."

"That's true. Then she would've probably tried to make it look like an accident, for insurance purposes if nothing else."

"Why would that affect the insurance?"

"Many life insurance policies have a double indemnity clause that pays the family twice as much if the victim dies in an accident, and a murderer can't collect on the victim's life insurance."

"If the wife didn't kill him, do you think we'll find her sitting in the condo?"

"My fear is we're going to find her body in the condo."

The gravity of my words hit Rachel. "Oh. We'll have to get a warrant to go inside to check on her?"

"If she was killed at the same time as her husband, we'll know pretty quickly. That's if the neighbors haven't already complained about the smell."

We rode in silence the rest of the way to the condo, while Rachel pondered what we might find.

* * *

Aransas Wharf was a thirty-story condo building overlooking the Gulf of Mexico. Like all of Mustang Island, it had taken a direct hit from Hurricane Harvey in 2017. The hurricane eye crossed over Rockport, thirty miles north, but Mustang Island had been decimated by the westerly winds on the backside of the eye. Most of the Mustang Island hotels and condos were made of cement with hurricane shutters facing east, toward the Gulf of Mexico. They were structurally sound, but west-facing windows and doors had been broken, and water had flowed through virtually all the condo buildings. Aransas Wharf still had a few doors covered with plywood, awaiting insurance payments, available craftsmen, or someone to buy the condo from the bank after the owners walked away from their mortgage.

The manager's office was on the first floor behind a new glass door that still had the manufacturer's stickers on the glass. A man wearing a Hawaiian print shirt sat in a lawn chair with nylon webbing behind a makeshift desk made from a sheet of plywood set on two sawhorses. He looked up from his computer, visibly surprised to see Rachel's Park Service uniform.

I handed him my badge and I.D.

"Help you" He had a deep south Texas accent.

"I'd like to know about one of your owners."

He studied my I.D.

"Ted Kaplan owns a condo here, right?" I studied his lined face. He'd spent a lot of his seventy-odd years in the sun, and I surmised this was his retirement job. There was a faded U.S.M.C. tattoo on his left forearm, and he wore his hair in a gray military buzz cut.

"Sure. We've got a Kaplan. What about him."

"Is Mrs. Kaplan in the condo?"

He handed my badge back. "Don't know. Not my job to keep track of the comings and goings of the owners."

"Did you see Mr. Kaplan last weekend?"

"Haven't seen him since the hurricane."

"How about Wendy Kaplan?" Rachel asked. "When did you see her last?"

"Hard to say."

I folded my ID case and put it in my pocket. "Guess."

"Last week sometime, I s'pose."

"We need to see if Mrs. Kaplan is alive, sergeant. Can you let us in their condo?"

I saw the flicker in his eyes when I addressed him as sergeant. "You look Army."

"Doug Fletcher, MPs. SFC when I mustered out after one tour in Iraq."

The manager offered his hand. "Ken Pollock. Master Gunny. Three tours in Nam."

Rachel watched with amusement as we established our military credentials.

"Why wouldn't Wendy Kaplan be okay?"

"Ted Kaplan's body washed up on North Padre Island and we're concerned about her welfare."

Pollock's eyes widened. "Ted's dead?"

"We watched his autopsy yesterday. Looks like he drowned in a bathtub."

"You're thinking this bathtub?"

"That's what we hope to find out. That, and to see if Wendy Kaplan is still alive. Have you seen her today?"

"I haven't seen her in a couple days, now you mention it." Pollock picked up a large keyring from the plywood tabletop, led us to an elevator, and pushed the call button. The door opened, and he pushed the button for the twenty-eighth floor.

"Have any of the neighbors complained about a smell coming from the apartment?"

Pollock shook his head. "No smell complaints."

"Any noise complaints last week?"

"Naw," Pollock said, holding the elevator door for us. "This is a pretty quiet place. Most of the condos are permanent owners who come here from Central Texas in the summer to escape the heat. We get some Northerners

199

renting in the winter. Most are disappointed it's not as warm as South Padre Island and sell after a couple trips. Right now, there aren't many people around."

He led us to condo number 2812 and knocked on the door. He stepped aside when I pulled back my shirttail and put my hand on the butt of the Sig pistol.

Rachel sniffed at the hinge side of the door. "I don't smell anything."

I knocked harder on the door. "Police!"

When no one answered, I looked at Pollock's keyring. "Are you going to make us get a search warrant, or will you help us do a wellness check on Wendy Kaplan?"

Pollock considered my question. "You're no average Park Service Ranger or former MP. You're a real cop."

"I was a detective, then I joined the Park Service." I wiggled my fingers for the keys.

"So, you look for Wendy, don't touch anything, and if she's okay, or not here, you leave. Right?"

"Right."

He sorted through the keys, found a master, and handed it to me.

"What's the layout?"

"Long hallway straight ahead, leading to the living room. There's a laundry room on the left as soon as you open the door and an alcove on the right leading to the guest bathroom and bedroom. The master suite is left, off the living room. Kitchen on the right. There's a balcony overlooking the gulf across the living room and master bedroom."

I drew my Sig and looked at Rachel, whose eyes grew wide. I nodded to her and slipped off the safety before unlocking the door.

Rachel drew her Sig and looked terrified. She whispered, "We're not wearing vests."

"There's probably no one inside."

She looked increasingly anxious. "How about calling for backup?"

I paused and assessed her anxiety. "You've never made an armed entry before, have you?"

She shook her head. "We talked about them."

I looked at Pollock as he reached behind his back and drew a Glock from under his shirttail. "Really?" I asked him.

"Hey, it's Texas. Everyone carries here."

I shook my head. "I'm not making an entry with a civilian."

We looked at Rachel, who appeared overwhelmed. Pollock put his hand on the doorknob. "It's just like breaching a hooch. I'll push the door. You go low left, and I'll go high right."

Rachel shook her head. "Wait. I'll call Corpus Christi PD and get a car out here."

Pollock pushed the door open and gave me a shove to the left. "Laundry is clear."

Chapter 17

Rachel stood frozen in the doorway when I looked over my shoulder.

I nodded at her. "The kitchen."

She slipped off the Sig's safety and moved down the hallway like she expected someone to jump out and yell, "Boo!"

"Guest bedroom is clear," Pollock yelled, before meeting me in the hallway.

Rachel stopped at the kitchen, sweeping her pistol back and forth across the small empty space.

I slid past her and scanned the empty living room before going left into the master bedroom. Pollock was behind me and went into the bathroom.

The bed was unmade, and there were clothes strewn on the floor. Pollock came out of the bathroom and slipped the Glock into the holster in the small of his back.

Rachel peeked around the bedroom door. "Are we done?"

I holstered my weapon. "It's clear. Looks like the bed's been used recently, and somebody's been shooting up." I pointed at the syringe, tubing, spoon, lighter, and cotton ball on the bedside table.

"Shooting up?" Rachel asked as she used both hands to hold her pistol while she put the safety on.

"Probably heroin or coke."

"Bathroom's a fucking mess." Pollock led us past a walk-in closet filled with men's and women's clothing, then into the master bathroom. There was a double sink, a toilet, a shower, and a bathtub. The marble floor was strewn with men's clothing and bloody towels, along with some plastic cable ties. There was blood smeared on the tile over the tub and on wet towels inside the tub. The cleaning effort had been brief and ineffective.

Rachel looked stricken. "Wendy Kaplan's not here. We have to leave."

I nodded, but Pollock looked troubled. "What're you thinking, Gunny?"

"We can't just walk away. This is a crime scene."

"We'll lock up and call the local police. They can get a warrant."

Pollock studied the dresser behind me. I'd noticed two of the drawers were open. He pointed to the compact video camera sitting on top. "I don't suppose you could peek at whatever's on the video camera?"

"We can't. It'll have to wait for a warrant."

Pollock shook his head. "The law really handcuffs you, doesn't it?"

Rachel was recovering and holstered her gun. "The courts want to make sure everyone's rights are protected."

"I kinda like the saying we had back in Nam. 'Shoot 'em all and let God sort them out.'"

I gestured for him to leave. "Those days are gone." We walked out, and Pollock locked the door.

"Has Wendy Kaplan had any visitors?"

Pollock pushed the elevator call button. "Here's where my ethics get tried. I'm paid to be blind unless someone's damaging the common property or breaking into a condo."

"So, you can't say if Wendy Kaplan was here with someone, or you don't know?"

Pollock pushed the elevator call button again like it would speed the response. "Tell you what, I didn't see a thing, but there are security cameras in the lobby and each hallway. I might be able to show you the security recordings without compromising my responsibilities."

"Does your tape loop and re-record over previous periods?"

Pollock shook his head. "You're a cop of the eighties. We got new equipment after Harvey. It's all digital, and the storage is in the cloud."

Rachel read my lack of understanding. "That means the storage is remote and nearly infinite."

Pollock led us to a closet off the lobby where a monitor displayed the lobby. He sat in a folding chair and typed commands into a computer. "Here's the lobby view for the past week." He winked at me. "Not that I know that's the timeframe you need to check."

At high speed, we watched the empty lobby, then people flashed by, going to the office or the elevator. The time and date flashed on the bottom of the frame. When the dates showed the weekend, Pollock slowed the speed whenever we saw activity. Each time people showed up, we looked at the faces, then went back to fast forward. Pollock stopped the recording when a woman and two men appeared.

Pollock pointed to the screen. "That's Wendy Kaplan."

"Do you recognize the men?"

"They've been hanging around with her for a few days. She never introduced them, and I never asked. I'd just saw them walk past the office on the way to the elevator."

He switched the view to the camera on the twenty-eighth floor. We watched the elevator door open, and the threesome walked to Kaplan's condo. Wendy stood by the door as one of the men pulled the keys out of his pocket and unlocked it.

"Interesting, that the man had her key."

Rachel pointed at the screen. "She's not right."

"What do you mean?" I asked.

"She looks spaced out and wobbly. Did you notice how she stumbled coming out of the elevator? And she doesn't look comfortable."

I looked at Pollock, who was studying the video. "What do you think?"

"We're not looking at the happy-go-lucky Wendy Kaplan I usually see when she's here with her husband. She's usually all smiles and talking all the time. Doesn't look like she's saying a word."

I nodded my understanding. "Let's watch the lobby to see when they leave."

Pollock sped up the replay, and we watched a few people come and leave, then he froze the replay and ran it back. "Whoa. I think that's Ted Kaplan."

The frame said the video had been recorded at 4:43 a.m. Monday. Ted Kaplan looked rumpled and tired, standing in front of the elevator doors. He walked into the elevator, and Pollock switched to the twenty-eighth floor. We watched Kaplan leave the elevator, walk to the condo, unlock the door, and step inside.

"Too bad we don't have any audio," Pollock said as he gave me a disgusted look. Then he sped up the playback. At 7:12 a.m., we watched the two men who arrived with Wendy Kaplan walk out of the condo carrying a rug that might've been wrapped around a body.

"I don't suppose you have video of the parking lot, so we know what kind of vehicle they put the rug in."

Pollock typed a command into the keyboard, and we watched the empty parking lot until the two men came out and placed the rug into the rear of a Honda minivan.

Rachel leaned close. "Do you suppose that's Mr. or Mrs. Kaplan?"

Pollock leaned back. "That's not two bodies. My bet is it's Ted."

I pointed at the back of the minivan. "Can you get the license number?"

Pollock enlarged the image, but the digits just got hazy. "I can't make them legible."

I shook my head. "That would've been almost too much to hope for. Please secure the video, and the condo until we get back with a search warrant."

Pollock typed in a command, and the video switched to a live view of the parking lot. "Are you talking yet today, Fletcher? I'm only on until five."

"Which city has jurisdiction here?"

"We're south of Port Aransas, so we're inside the Corpus Christi city limits. That said, I see Nueces County cops more than I see Corpus Christi police patrolling the highway."

"I'll call Corpus Christi. I suspect they'd be interested in investigating a murder inside the city limits."

Pollock checked his watch. "If you want the condo watched after five, you'll have to get someone out here to sit in the hallway."

We walked back to the Park Service pickup. "Can you get a non-emergency number for the Corpus Christi PD on your smartphone, Rachel?"

"Sure. Do you want to explain what's going on?"

We sat in the pickup with the windows down. It took nearly ten minutes, a dropped call, and three transfers before I spoke with Scott Dixon, a detective with the CCPD. I introduced myself and explained the recovery of Kaplan's body, the identification, and locating Kaplan's condo.

"Have you already been inside the condo?"

"We made a safety check on Wendy Kaplan. We had reason to believe she might be in danger."

"Did you touch anything?"

"I'm an investigator with the Park Service, and I spent nearly twenty years as a St. Paul cop and detective. I know the law, and I know not to screw up evidence. We backed out as soon as we determined the apartment was a crime scene."

The phone went silent for a moment while Dixon considered my words. "So, it looks like a murder scene, and there's no sign of the wife?"

"Right. There's drug paraphernalia on the nightstand, and we watched the condo video surveillance showing Ted Kaplan arriving, then two men carrying out what appears to be a body wrapped in a rug. We spoke with the husband's office, and Wendy Kaplan is out of touch. The condo manager identified her on video taken before Ted Kaplan's arrival, then leaving with the two men who carried out the body."

"And the wife is missing?"

"Yes. The condo manager said he hasn't seen her for a couple days."

"Well, hell. It sounds like you've just dumped a murder and possible kidnapping in my lap. I suppose I'll have to get a search warrant and use your questionable search as probable cause."

"There's one other thing. Kaplan is a prosecutor for Hennepin County, in Minneapolis. He missed the opening comments of a drug case on Monday."

"That sounds like motive to me. Give me your cellphone number, and I'll see how quickly I can get a search warrant."

After I gave him the info, I handed the phone back to Rachel, who disconnected the call. "Does that mean we're done?"

"I think we need to hang around until detective Dixon shows up. Maybe he'll let us come along on his search."

Rachel silently stared out the windshield, apparently deep in thought.

"What's wrong?" I asked.

"You and the building manager were absolutely fearless. You walked into that apartment and cleared room after room without blinking an eye."

"We knocked, and there was no response. Pollock knew no one was home."

"I wasn't sure of that. And I was scared spitless. There was no way I could've gone in there as your backup. My feet weren't ready to move when you said, 'clear the kitchen.' In my classes, they said we'd never make an entry without an entry team in helmets and tactical vests. You didn't even have a light vest."

"Like I said, the condo was empty. We weren't in danger."

"You went in with your gun drawn," she countered.

"That's just common sense. There's always a small chance you're not as smart as you think you are. That's why you should be ready to draw your gun during every traffic stop. You never know when a driver is going to poke a gun out the window and start shooting at you."

"That doesn't happen in the parks."

"It happened on Phoenix highways twice last week, and who's to say the nut you're pulling over isn't escaping from a chase that got called off. Be ready to draw and shoot in every encounter."

"I can't walk up to a car with two parents and a bunch of kids with my gun drawn."

"You shouldn't have your gun drawn, but you need to be mentally prepared for the unthinkable possibility that Daddy is a crackhead and will point a gun at your face when you ask for his driver's license."

"That's not likely."

"You've got to be prepared for that one in a thousand times when it happens. The one time you're not, might be the one time when you needed to be prepared. Your mental state might mean the difference between a scary situation and a trip in the back of an ambulance."

"Or to the morgue," Rachel said, the gravity of our conversation hitting home.

"When I was a St. Paul cop, my training officer told me you don't need your gun until you need it badly."

"You said that before." She paused. "I heard you were in a shootout in Flagstaff. How scary was it?"

"I didn't have time to be scared. And, I wasn't really in a shootout. By the time I got my Sig out of the holster, it was over."

"How many shots were fired?"

"Nine, I think."

"Nine shots were fired before you could get your gun out? That's scary as hell."

"Yes, it is. Glock advertises that their guns can fire eighteen shots in nine seconds."

"You can't hit anything shooting that fast."

"There was an Army sniper in Viet Nam who killed nineteen Viet Cong soldiers in ten seconds."

"With a machine gun."

"With nineteen aimed shots from an M-14 rifle. I saw an instructor duplicate that feat shooting balloons on a firing range."

She studied my face. "You're serious."

"I'm deadly serious. You've got to know how to use your weapon, and you've got to be prepared to use it. Glock's law enforcement literature sums it up nicely. 'When you leave for work you should have one goal—getting home.'"

My cellphone trilled while Rachel considered that. "Fletcher."

"This is Dixon. I've got a warrant. Are you still at Aransas Wharf?"

"We're parked in the lot. How long before you can get here?"

"I'm on the road. I should be there in ten minutes if I don't hit traffic."

"We'll have the superintendent cue up the video, and we'll meet you in the lobby."

Chapter 18

Rachel and I were talking to Pollock when an unmarked car pulled into the lot. Dixon parked in the fire lane in front of the office. He was tall, wearing jeans, a western cut shirt, cowboy boots, and a white hat. He wore a badge on his belt and a pistol on his left hip. He walked down the sidewalk with a bow-legged swagger like he'd just got off his horse.

"Dixon?" I asked, offering my hand.

"You're dressed mighty casual for a Park Ranger." He shook my hand. He appraised my khaki pants and casual shirt, pausing at the badge and holster clipped to my belt. He made me feel like I should buy some cowboy boots and a shirt with pearl buttons to fit in.

"This is my partner, Rachel Randall."

"*You* actually look like a Park Ranger." Rachel was in uniform, from her Smokey Bear hat to gray shirt and green pants. She had her badge pinned to her shirt and wore a "duty belt" with holster, spare magazines for her pistol, mace, and handcuffs.

"Do you want to start by looking at the images from the security cameras?" I asked.

"Sure," Dixon replied.

Pollock watched us through the windows. He shut down his computer and met us at the door.

I introduced Dixon to Pollock. "The video equipment is set up in the other room. I cued up the recording to Wendy Kaplan arriving with the two men."

We watched the two men and Wendy Kaplan enter the lobby, then switched to the video of them outside the condo. Pollock moved the replay ahead to Ted Kaplan entering, then jumped ahead to the two guys carrying out the rug and driving away. They came back two hours later and went back to the Kaplan condo. We watched Wendy walk out with the two men shortly after their return.

"That's it." Pollock handed a CD to Dixon.

"Is this the original?"

"It's complicated," Pollock explained. "The video storage is in the cloud, and I made a copy. Do you have a search warrant for the condo?"

Dixon pulled the search warrant from his back pocket and unfolded it. Pollock took the paper and looked it over. "Okay if I make a copy for my files?"

"Have at it." As Pollock made a copy, Dixon took us aside. "So, what's upstairs?"

"The condo looks lived in. There are clothes on the floor and dirty dishes in the sink. It looks like the residents left fast. There's a heroin kit on the nightstand, bloody towels in the bathtub, and a video camera on the dresser. We didn't touch any of it. As soon as we

214

determined Wendy Kaplan wasn't there, we backed out and locked the apartment."

"Who authorized you to look for Wendy?"

"I spoke with the Hennepin County Attorney, and he asked me to check on Wendy. She didn't answer the door. I asked the super to open the door, so we could check on her. I suspected we might find her body."

"You didn't look at the video on the camera?"

Pollock handed the search warrant back to Dixon. "No, they didn't. I was with them. They checked all the rooms for Mrs. Kaplan, we backed out, then I locked the condo, and I've been watching it ever since."

"No one's been in the condo since then?" Dixon asked.

Pollock shook his head. "I've been here in the lobby, and there have only been five people through. None of them stopped on the twenty-eighth floor. I can pull up the video feed for the last three hours if you'd like."

"Let's look in the condo." Dixon handed us each a pair of purple nitrile gloves as we rode the elevator. "Don't touch anything."

Pollock unlocked the door, and Dixon hesitated. "I'd like Fletcher to come inside with me. You two wait outside, so we don't contaminate the scene any more than necessary."

I went in with Dixon, who ambled past the laundry room and guest suite with his hand on the butt of his pistol. He stopped at the kitchen and looked at the dishes on the counter and in the sink. There was a slight odor of rotting food and mold. The living room was unremarkable aside from the beer cans and glasses sitting on the coffee and end tables. There was a laptop computer on the table in the dining area and a briefcase on the floor.

Dixon nodded his chin toward the living room. "We ought to be able to pull prints and DNA off of the dishes and cans if we think this is a crime scene."

We stopped at the bedroom door and took in the view. I pointed to the drug paraphernalia. "Heroin?"

"Hard to say. We've got people shooting up all kinds of shit, from heroin to cocaine and meth. It's safest to let the experts do the testing."

Dixon stopped at the walk-in closet. "Looks like a couple lived here."

He stopped at the bathroom door and studied the scene. "Did the body you recovered have ligatures?"

"He still had cable ties on his wrists and ankles when we recovered the body. I imagine your forensic people would be able to tell us if they're the same as these."

"There's not a lot of blood here. What was your victim's cause of death?"

"Drowning in freshwater. There were traces of chlorine and fluoride in the water, so the medical examiner speculated he'd drowned in city water, like in a bathtub."

"Let's see if there's anything in the recorder memory."

I followed Dixon to the bedroom, and he picked up the camera in his gloved hands. He turned it on and paged through screens to get to the memory. He selected the most recent video, and the tiny screen displayed a couple having sex on the bed. The shadowbox over the head of the bed in the video matched the one in the room.

Dixon turned the camera so I could see the small screen. "Can you tell if it's the same woman who was on the security camera?" I shook my head.

We watched for a few more seconds, then he went back to the memory and selected a different video. The next video showed the woman, wearing panties and a bra, bound to the bedframe. A man, with his back to the camera, tied a rubber band around the woman's arm while she struggled against the restraints. There was a muffled, unintelligible conversation that sounded like the woman begging. We watched the man draw liquid into a syringe, then pin the woman's arm with one hand and plunge the needle into a vein. The woman screamed, "No!" as the syringe plunger was pushed. The man removed the needle and released the rubber band while the woman sobbed.

"Doesn't appear she was a willing participant in whatever happened." Dixon shut off the camera. He put it back on the dresser, and we walked into the living room.

"I assume your department has some forensic computer guys who'll be able to see what's on the laptop."

Dixon took a deep breath and surveyed the room. "Yeah, I'll get a forensics team over here and have them go through everything, including the laptop. As for the wife, I don't think there's a lot of hope she's still alive. I suppose they used her to get her husband down here, and once she wasn't useful anymore, they probably killed her."

"I'll call Kaplan's boss, the county prosecutor, and update him."

Dixon pulled out his smartphone "Give me his number. I need to talk to him about the husband and what he was into. I'll fill him in on the wife's situation. Remind me of their names."

"They were Ted and Wendy Kaplan." I paused while he put the names into his phone. "I hope you can pull some prints off the cans and glasses. Maybe you'll be able to find the guys in the video. They might be keeping her alive for entertainment."

Dixon shook his head. "She might be better off dead than drugged up for a week or more and used like a whore."

"Or sold to the cartels," I added.

Rachel and Pollock met us at the door. Rachel looked stricken. "Was Wendy Kaplan on the video?"

"I'm afraid so."

Pollock shook his head. "God, what a shame. She's a nice pretty gal. It'd be a shame to see her drugged up and abused."

Rachel looked between Dixon and me. "We have to find her! What are we going to do?"

Dixon pulled out his phone and punched in a number. "Dale? Hey, it's Scott. There's a condo here, and the bathroom and bedroom are crime scenes. The husband was probably killed here, and the wife has been drugged and kidnapped." He listened for a moment. "I'll text the address to you with the details about the wife."

After ending his call, he looked at Rachel. "We're going to jump on this. But, let me be clear, this is my case, not yours. As a professional courtesy, I'll keep Fletcher updated on what's happening. But I want you guys to step away from this and let us handle it. Are we clear on that?"

I nodded, but Rachel was agitated. "No way! If there's anything we can do, I'll be pursuing it."

"Ma'am, I'm going to say this as politely as I can. Stand down. It's not your case."

"It's an interstate kidnapping case. I'll call the FBI!"

Dixon glanced at me, and I shook my head. "No, Rachel. If Detective Dixon feels he needs the assistance of the FBI, he can call them. It's not our case. We have to let him do his job, and we need to stay out of his way."

"But the FBI…"

I shook my head. "There is a time and place to call in the FBI, but this isn't it. Besides, my experiences with the FBI haven't been entirely positive."

Dixon snorted. "I don't know any investigator who's been happy about having the FBI step into their investigation."

Rachel asked, looking between us. "What do you mean?"

"When the FBI gets involved, we lose control," Dixon explained. "We're better off handling this locally, where I can expedite the forensic testing, and we can use our local resources to find the wife. If the FBI gets involved, all the evidence will go to their labs, where it will get in queue behind every other major crime they have across the nation. They'll send in agents who don't know Corpus Christi and who don't have informants or resources here. All they'll do is slow things down."

I nodded. "In the end, they'll either take responsibility for solving the case, or they'll quietly leave and throw everything back in detective Dixon's lap."

"You make them sound like glory hounds."

"And you, ma'am, have been watching too much television and have too little experience." Dixon handed us each a business card. "We're done here until the forensics team shows up. I need a key to the apartment and access to the security videos."

Pollock pulled the door closed and locked it. "I have a spare master downstairs." He led us to the elevator. "Ms. Kaplan was doped up?"

I nodded. "It appears so."

"I feel just terrible," Pollock said as we stepped into the elevator. "I wish I'd known. I could've..."

Dixon handed Pollock a business card. "You've never seen the two men who were with her before?"

Pollock shook his head as we stepped into the elevator. "I kinda figured maybe they were people she knew from Minnesota."

Dixon pushed the button for the ground floor. "Any chance it's someone she'd met in a local bar?"

"I'm paid to be discreet. If she met some folks and they were all being friendly, it's not my place to interrogate them."

"Let's hope my forensics people can pick up a fingerprint and enhance the security camera images so we can get the license number of the Honda minivan."

Rachel wasn't satisfied with Dixon's methodical approach to the case. "In the meanwhile, what's happening to Wendy Kaplan?"

Dixon looked pained. "There's nothin' I can do until I can identify the guys who were with her. I hate to think about what's happening to her if she's still alive, but there's nothing to be done until then."

Rachel was indignant. "That sucks!"

Dixon looked at me for support. I added, "It sucks, but Detective Dixon is doing all the right things, and he's promised to expedite the forensic testing."

Pollock shook his head. "It's FUBAR, but I don't know what else he can do."

"FUBAR?" Rachel asked.

"It's an old Marine Corps acronym: Fucked up beyond all recognition."

Rachel glared at all three of us and stalked to the pickup.

Dixon looked at me. "Are you going to be able to keep her from nosing around in this?"

"I don't know what she could do. Without the forensics, we're hamstrung."

Pollock jammed his hands into his jean pockets. "I've got some contacts in the community. I can call around and see if anyone's seen the minivan in the security footage with two men and a woman in it. Maybe they're checked into a hotel somewhere nearby."

Dixon looked skeptical. "If you do, tell me what you find out. Don't go playing John Wayne. Understood?"

"Yes, sir."

"You were an NCO in the Corps?" Dixon asked.

"Master gunny with thirty-two years in, sir."

Dixon smiled. "Thank you for your service, Gunny. You don't need to call me, sir. I was a lowly lance corporal when my enlistment was up."

Pollock smiled. "In that case, you go find Ms. Kaplan, or I'm going to kick your ass like a drill instructor."

"Aye, aye, Gunny." Dixon turned to me. "Where's Ted Kaplan's body?"

"It's in the Corpus Christi hospital morgue."

"Gunny, I'd like to use your landline to make a few calls."

I walked to the pickup and climbed inside.

Rachel's head was down, and she appeared to be rooted in thought. "Let's stop at the gas stations on the way to Corpus Christi and see if any of them have security video of those guys."

"Dixon's people will be doing that. And, he told us to stay out of his investigation."

She glared at me. "Matt Mattson told me you are a maverick who got things done."

"So, you want me to risk a reprimand by interfering with Dixon's investigation?"

"One of my instructors said, 'It's better to ask forgiveness for doing what you know is right than to ask permission when you know the answer will be no.'"

I started the pickup and turned onto the highway toward Packery Channel, the waterway separating Mustang Island from North Padre Island. "Looks like we're a little low on gas. I'll fill up at the corner. Why don't you go inside and ask about their security camera footage?"

"So, you're just gassing up the truck, and I'm sticking my neck out by asking about security camera recordings."

"You're the one who suggested we go to the gas station. You should have the honor of discovering the missing link in the investigation if it's here."

"I'll do that if you give me twenty bucks for a couple burgers and sodas."

"Why am I buying you lunch?"

"Because it's late afternoon, I'm hungry, my lunch is sitting in the refrigerator at the visitor center break room, and because you're a highly paid investigator and I'm a lowly ranger."

I pulled up to the gas pumps and handed Rachel a twenty-dollar bill. Then I pulled out my government credit card and filled the gas tank. When Rachel didn't return, I moved the pickup to a parking spot and walked inside. The gas station was also a convenience store where tourists could buy basic groceries. There was a cooler full of sandwiches, and some sausages were rolling on a heater next to a counter filled with condiments. Rachel stood in front of a humming microwave. There was a wrapper in a paper tray. When the microwave dinged, she pulled out a steaming hamburger and handed it to me.

"I poured sweet tea for us and put the cups on the table." She pointed.

I saw two foam cups sitting on one of the four small tables. I put ketchup and mustard on a pathetic looking burger with a soggy bun. An immense man wearing a Kenworth truck cap and bib overalls sat on the other side of the narrow aisle. He wolfed down a sausage in a bun while grease and mustard leaked out, dribbling onto a second sausage laying in a second paper tray. He nodded to me, and I nodded back.

Rachel slid into the chair across from me, and I noticed the trucker checking out her backside. His eyes met mine, and he raised his eyebrows like he thought we were an item. I shook my head and looked away. When I glanced back, he smiled like he thought I was lying.

I watched Rachel push ketchup around her burger with a plastic stir stick. "I thought you were vegan."

"Toby is vegan. I'm omnivorous."

"I've heard that vegan people can smell meat in the sweat of carnivorous people."

"If he can, Toby's never said anything."

"Maybe the marijuana smoke dulls his sense of smell. Jill smelled it in his hair when he hugged her."

Rachel turned red but didn't respond.

"Did you ask about the security tapes?"

"The manager is burning a copy for me. We can take it back to the visitor center and look at it on a computer."

Chapter 19

Wendy Kaplan was nauseated, and that was an improvement from the stupor of the previous days. She looked around at the unfamiliar motel room, unable to remember arriving there. Her body wouldn't stop trembling, and her momentary mental acuity disintegrated into an overwhelming urge to find someone who could make her feel better. A basal instinct made her want something. She looked at the spoon, rubber tubing, syringe, empty glassine envelopes, and cotton ball on the bedside table. She licked her finger and wiped at the residue inside the bags, then her focus flicked to accessing a drop of liquid out of the cotton ball and into the syringe. A man walked in, and her first reaction was to recoil into a fetal position and cover her head. Her second reaction was to see if he had what she needed.

"Are you looking for this?" Digger asked, holding up a tiny glassine "stamp bag" containing grayish powder.

Wendy fixated on the bag.

"Merrill went out to get Chinese for supper, but I imagine you're more interested in shooting up than you are in egg rolls and moo goo gai pan." Digger sat on the edge of the bed and sprinkled the gray powder into the spoon. "I'm going to fix a hit for you, but I expect something in return."

"What?" Wendy asked, surprised at how raspy her voice was like she hadn't had a drink of water for days. She slid to the edge of the mattress next to Digger until their hips touched. He was an ugly man with ragged, dirty fingernails. A hairy back and shoulders showed from under his wife-beater tank top. He smelled like sweat and cigarettes. His fingers and teeth were stained yellow by nicotine.

"A woman like you wouldn't have had anything to do with me," Digger said as he added a few drops of water to the spoon, then poured in the powder. "But this little cocktail kinda levels the playing field, doesn't it?"

Wendy licked her lips, focused only on the spoon and the liquid Digger heated over a butane lighter. She grabbed the rubber tubing from the nightstand and cinched it tight around her upper arm, making her veins bulge and paying no notice to the "tracks" left by the previous injections.

Digger placed the cotton ball in the hot heroin mixture and drew the liquid through the cotton and into the syringe. Then he put the syringe on the table. Wendy craned her neck, looking around his shoulder to see why he'd stopped.

"Slip off your shirt and pants," Digger said. When Wendy hesitated, Digger added, "The quicker we get through this, the quicker you get your hit."

Wendy paused one more second, and then quickly pulled the t-shirt over her head.

Digger grabbed her breasts, squeezing them hard.

"Ouch!"

"I'm just playing with you a little. Now, pull those jeans off."

Wendy faltered but quietly complied. Then she laid back on the bed and watched Digger unbuckle his belt.

"What the hell are you doing?" Merrill asked from the door. His hands were filled with plastic bags full of take-out containers.

Digger held his pants up with one hand. "We were just about to have some fun."

"What's in the syringe?" Merrill set the bags down. "I didn't leave any horse here."

"I shorted a bundle by one bag. That junkie won't notice."

Merrill crossed the room and picked up the stamp bag, studying the blue logo printed on it. "This is the Mexican stuff laced with Fentanyl. It could kill her."

Digger smiled. "She'll never know what hit her, and I'll have a little fun before her heart stops."

Merrill picked up the syringe and pretended to examine the liquid. He jabbed it into Digger's muscular shoulder, driving the plunger home in one move.

"Jeez!" Digger grabbed the syringe and pulled it out of his shoulder. "What the hell?"

"How will a shot of Fentanyl affect you?"

Digger felt the rush of the drugs as they hit his brain. "Get the Narcan."

"I haven't got any."

"Call for an EMT. They carry Narcan."

Wendy, sitting naked on the bed, watched with horror as Digger collapsed next to her on the mattress.

Merrill looked at the fresh welts on her bruised breasts and shook his head. There was blood on the sheets and her legs. "Did he hurt you?"

Wendy looked down. "Um, no. I think I need a new tampon."

"Get your clothes on."

She scrambled into her jeans and shirt like an obedient child. The clothes hung on her— after days on drugs she'd lost interest in eating.

Digger convulsed and vomited, causing Wendy to jump aside. He rolled on his back and aspirated on his own vomit, slowly choking to death as Wendy tied her shoes.

* * *

Merrill pulled to the curb and reached across Wendy Kaplan's lap, unlatched the door, and pushed it open. "Get out."

"What?" Wendy looked around at the urban neighborhood with confusion.

"Get out of the car. You're not coming with me any farther."

"Here?" She looked at him, then glanced at the small carryon bag and licked her dry lips. "I need a bump."

Merrill unlatched her seatbelt and shoved her. "There's no more. Get out."

Wendy stumbled to the curb and watched the minivan's taillights disappear down the street and turn at the corner. She studied the mostly industrial neighborhood, trying to decide what to do. Bright lights down the block drew her like a moth, and she stumbled down the sidewalk until she saw the red Emergency Room logo over a sliding glass door.

Wendy walked into the emergency room in a daze. People were dispersed around the room, some alone and others in small groups. Some were coughing. Others were moaning. One man was holding a bloody towel wrapped around his hand.

"Can I help you?" a matronly Hispanic woman asked from behind a desk. She had a pleasant smile, and her name badge said she was Angelique, a volunteer.

"I'm...not sure."

"What's the matter, Miss?"

Wendy felt chilled, and her body tremored. "I...maybe I'll leave."

"You're drenched with sweat, and you've got goosebumps. Do you have a fever?"

Wendy wrapped her arms around herself and shivered. "I don't think so."

"You sit down here for a minute." Angelique pointed to a chair facing her desk. "I'll be right back."

Wendy sat down and bent over as her stomach spasmed. Angelique returned after several minutes with a woman carrying a clipboard.

"I need you to fill out some forms for me." A laminated badge hanging from a lanyard said she was an admitting clerk named Wanda. She was chubby, middle-aged, and harried.

"I think I'll just go." Wendy teetered when she stood, and Angelique rushed to her side, helping her sit in the chair.

Angelique shooed Wanda away. "Leave the forms. I'll help her."

Wanda seemed to be relieved and left the clipboard, hustling back through a door behind a security officer.

"What's your name?"

"Wendy. Wendy Kaplan."

"Where do you live?"

"Um, in Minnesota."

Angelique looked at Wendy and thought she was too old to be a runaway. "Do you have an address there?" Wendy recited her street address, city, state, and zip code, and Angelique wrote them down. "Do you have a driver's license and insurance card?"

Wendy shook her head. "I guess I lost them. I think my husband has Blue Cross insurance."

It took nearly fifteen minutes for Angelique to get Wendy Kaplan's health insurance information. The longer Angelique was on the phone, the more restless Wendy became.

Wendy stood up. "I'm going."

Angelique assessed the needle tracks on Wendy's arms. "Have you been taking drugs?"

"I have to go." Wendy became more insistent.

"Where are you going?"

"Home, I think."

"You're in Texas. Home is a long way from here."

Wendy looked around the waiting area like she was seeing it for the first time. She was wracked by another bout of shivers and nearly fell into the chair. "Call my husband. He'll come and get me."

"What's the phone number?"

Wendy recited her home phone number. Angelique dialed it and left a message at the tone. "Is there a different number I can call?"

"Try Ted's cellphone." She recited a different number.

After Angelique left messages at every Twin Cities phone number Wendy could remember, she gave Angelique a number with a Wisconsin area code. Wendy's mother answered her cellphone. "Hello, this is Angelique Ramos at the Corpus Christi Hospital emergency room. Wendy Kaplan is here, and I haven't been able to contact her husband."

"Wendy's in the hospital, in Texas?"

"She hasn't been admitted, but yes, she's here."

Angelique heard muted voices then a man's voice came on the line. "This is Wendy's father. What kind of scam are you running?"

"Sir, this is no scam. I'm a volunteer in the hospital emergency room and Wendy Kaplan walked in a while ago. I've just got her insurance information, but she says she wants to leave. Would you talk to her?"

"Sure."

Wendy accepted the phone reluctantly. "Hello."

"Who is this?" The man demanded.

"Daddy, it's Wendy. We can't find Ted. Can you come and get me?"

John Antonich nearly dropped the phone. "Wendy, where are you?"

"I don't know, but there's a nice woman here, and she's been trying to find Ted. I want to go home."

"Wendy, stay with the nice woman. I'll come and get you as soon as I can. okay?"

"I really need to leave. I feel…"

"Put the nice woman back on the phone, Honey."

"This is Angelique."

"What's the matter with Wendy? Why is she in the emergency room?"

"I'm no doctor, but I'd say she's going through drug withdrawal."

"My God! Can you keep her there until I can get a flight?"

"Wendy's an adult, and I really can't compel her to stay here against her will. I can try to persuade her to stay and be treated, but if she walks away…"

"Her husband is missing, and we believe Wendy was kidnapped. If nothing else works, please call the local police and have them hold her."

Angelique looked at the security officer guarding the entrance to the treatment area. "I'll figure out something. Get yourself down here as fast as you can."

"Where, exactly, is here?" Antonich asked.

"Corpus Christi, Texas."

"I'll charter a plane if I have to. Just keep her safe until I arrive."

"I will," Angelique disconnected the call and dialed 911. "I have a woman here who we believe is a kidnapping victim. She's with me in the Corpus Christi emergency room…"

* * *

John Antonich dialed Ted Kaplan's number at the Hennepin County Attorney's office. His assistant, Janet Levi, answered the phone.

"This is John Antonich. Put Ted's boss on the phone right now."

"I'm sorry, sir. I can put you through to Mr. Parker's office, and I'm sure someone will be able to assist you."

"I'm Wendy Kaplan's father. She's been found in Texas, and I want to talk to the head man, now!"

"Oh! I'll transfer you to Mr. Parker's line."

"You'll do no such thing! You'll hustle to his office and tell him I'm on the phone, and I want to talk to him immediately."

"I'm sorry sir, but I don't even know if he's in the office today."

"Is his office nearby?"

"Well, yes. It's just a few doors down."

The tone in Antonich's voice left little room for interpretation. "Don't put me on hold. Just set the phone down and run to his office. Do you understand me?"

"Hang on."

"This is Roger Parker. What's your name, sir?"

"I'm John Antonich, Wendy Kaplan's father. Are you the county attorney that Ted works for?"

"Yes, Ted works in my office, I hope you…"

"Listen to me, Parker. Wendy is in a Texas emergency room. I'm in central Wisconsin, and I need to get to Texas ASAP. Do you have some political supporter who has a private plane that can get me to Corpus Christi, wherever the hell that is, in Texas."

"Our office doesn't have access to a private plane. We fly commercial…"

"I didn't ask if *you* had a plane. I asked you to get hold of one of your local politicos, who'd like to have you owe him a favor and ask him to put his plane in the air to the Appleton International Airport. I'll be waiting in the private aviation building by the time the plane gets there."

"Mr. Antonich, I'm afraid I don't have those kinds of contacts…"

"Damn it, Parker, you've been dancing around Wendy and Ted's disappearances for a week. With no help from you, I've finally located my daughter." Antonich paused. "Give me the phone number for your local newspaper. Is it the *Minneapolis Star* or something? I'm sure there's someone there who'd arrange a charter in return for an exclusive story."

"Hang on, Mr. Antonich. There's no need to get the news media involved in this. Let me make a few calls. Give me your phone number."

"Call my cellphone. I'll be at the damned airport. If there isn't a plane in the air by the time I get there, I'll book a private charter and be on the phone to the newspaper while they prep their plane."

"Give me a few minutes to make…" Parker realized he was listening to a dial tone. "Ashley! Get the governor on the phone, right now!"

Chapter 20

Rachel set up the television and CD player in the break room. I told her both of us didn't need to watch hours of useless video, so I went back to my office. I was mulling Dixon's order to stand down with my feet up on the desk drawer and a pencil in my hand. Something gnawed at me, but I couldn't get the thought out to the front of my brain where I could deal with it. I gave up and walked to Matt Mattson's office, interrupting his paperwork.

Matt took off a pair of reading glasses and looked up. "What did you find at the condo?"

I closed his office door. "We entered the condo to make a wellness check on Wendy Kaplan. I figured she was either dead or gone. Rachel was scared, not that being scared is a bad thing—when you stop being scared is when you do something stupid and get hurt. But she locked up. I'm sure she'll get past that, but it's going to take a while along with some self-confidence building before she is ready to deal with really bad people."

"I depend on you to make sure Rachel's learning the skills she needs and making sure she's safe."

"I'm doing my best, and she's trying, but it always takes some time for a rookie to get smart and confident. I think she's got the drive to get there. It's a little harder here than on the city streets because we're dealing with picnicking families who don't pose a lot of threat. A rookie cop in the city is going to see some pretty nasty situations very quickly. They grow up fast or quit."

"Speaking of that, there was a recent decision to allow people with 'carry permits' to enter the park with their concealed firearms."

"Seriously?"

"I think someone reasoned there are so many people who legally carry in Texas that it would be an enforcement nightmare to confiscate every firearm we saw. It's still illegal to discharge a firearm on Park Service property, but if you see someone with a gun tucked under their belt, it's okay."

"I warned Rachel about being ready for any traffic stop to devolve into a shooting situation."

"You told her to draw her gun when she's approaching a car she's pulled over?"

"No, I told her to be skeptical and approach every car as if the driver might point a gun at her and start shooting. I think that's prudent whether you're with Park Service or the Texas Rangers."

"It seems a little overboard for dealing with the people who come here."

"It's better to have a couple of uncomfortable confrontations with our visitors than for you to be rushing to a hospital because she's been shot."

Matt shifted in his chair, contemplating my words. "I suppose you're right, but it still seems a little over the top."

"Trust me. She needs to be prepared for the worst. I told her about my shootout in Arizona. There were nine shots fired before I could get my pistol out of my holster."

"That's hard to believe. I saw the report on your speed shooting prowess."

"Matt, most gunfights are over in eight seconds. If she's not prepared to pull her pistol to protect me, herself, or one of our visitors, someone could be badly injured, or dead."

"You're scaring me."

"Most cops retire without ever firing their weapons except on the range. But the reason they practice on the range is so that they're prepared if they need to draw their weapon."

"You said most cops don't fire their weapons. Is that a real statistic? Are you talking about fifty-one percent of them?"

"I'd say it's closer to ninety-eight percent who never fire a weapon at another person. That's probably a good estimate. The cops who shoot and kill someone are messed up for life. It's not easy to accept that you've taken another person's life. Whether you're a cop or a soldier, it weighs on you." I paused. "What branch of the service were you in?"

"Air Force. I was in for six years, including a year flying C-130s out of Bagram. I'm still in the Texas Air National Guard."

"Was anyone in your unit killed?"

"We were lucky. Everyone came home. But we flew a lot of critically wounded soldiers to Tempelhof for treatment in Germany. I walked into the back during each flight and shook hands with the real heroes. I went back to the cockpit with tears in my eyes every time."

"That could be Rachel or me if we're not vigilant and careful."

"Well, I can't say I'm glad we had this conversation." Matt got up from his chair, signaling the end of the conversation. He stood next to the door for a moment with his hand on the knob, obviously in thought. "You know, I'm glad you're here. Your experience brings a higher level of professionalism to our law enforcement effort. Thanks."

I walked out, and Matt closed the door.

Rachel stood in the hallway outside Matt's office. "Doug, do you have a minute?"

"Sure. What've you got?"

"I think a picture will be worth a thousand words." She led me down to the break room.

The television was frozen on a split image of a light-colored minivan at the gas pumps and the checkout counter inside. Rachel punched a button on the remote and the video played in jumps like it was taking a picture every second or two. A man stepped out of the minivan and moved to the gas pump. He inserted a charge card into the slot, then pumped gas. A second man stepped out, talked to the first man, then he went into the gas station. On the split-screen, I watched the man inside walk down an aisle where he took things off the shelf. The clerk took two packs of cigarettes out of a rack behind the counter, then rang up the man's purchase. When the gas purchase was completed, the outside man replaced the nozzle and screwed on the gas cap. The second man came out, opened the back door and handed part of his purchase to someone in the back seat, then he climbed into the front passenger seat.

"That's it," Rachel said, stopping the video. "I think they're the same guys from the condo, and now we know that Wendy Kaplan was still alive on Sunday, and they probably intended to keep her alive."

"How do we know that?"

"The guy bought Tampax. I doubt he'd be buying her tampons if they planned to kill her."

"You could tell that from the video?"

"The box is very distinctive."

"We've got to call Dixon. They'll be able to ID the driver. He used a credit card to pay for the gas at the pump. Good job!"

Rachel smiled. "I hadn't thought about the credit card. I was mostly pleased to see the tampon purchase and what it meant about Wendy Kaplan's situation."

"I hate to burst your bubble, but he could've been buying tampons for his girlfriend."

"I suppose that's a possibility."

I took Dixon's business card out of my wallet and walked to my office. I dialed his cellphone and punched the speakerphone button. "Scott, it's Doug Fletcher. I've got a video from a gas station security camera you need to see."

"I thought I told you guys to stand down."

"Have you been canvassing the gas stations and pulling their security video?"

"I'm with the forensics team at Kaplan's condo. So, no, I haven't gotten that far yet."

"Well, we happened to eat lunch at the first gas station on the island, and Rachel asked the manager if we could get a copy of the security video. She looked through the video and found pictures of the two guys who were with Wendy Kaplan at the condo. They used a credit card to pay for gas, and one guy went inside and bought tampons. So, we think Wendy is still alive. You should be able to get the credit card information on the driver."

"I'm up to my eyeballs right now."

"Dixon, say thank you."

The Corpus Christi detective took a deep breath and blew it out. "Thank you."

"Do you want to come here to watch the video, or would you like Rachel to bring it to you so you can cue it up yourself and look at the images of the two guys?"

"My people are wrapping up things here. Where are you?"

"We're in the break room at the Park Service headquarters building."

"I'll be there in half an hour."

"Do you want me to get the credit card number from the gas station?"

"Damn it, Fletcher, what part of 'stand-down' don't you understand?"

* * *

Rachel met Dixon at the gate and escorted him to the break room while I briefed Matt on her discovery. "I'd like to watch the video with you when the detective gets here," Matt said.

"I think that'd be a good idea. At some point, you're going to write up Rachel's review, and you need to give her credit for that great piece of police work."

Matt shook his head, smiling. "You're something else, Doug. Everyone else in the world is vying for credit for what they're doing or trying to take credit for what their peers are doing. You're passing out the credit and acting like you're an uninvolved observer."

"This is Rachel's work."

"Bullshit. I'll give Rachel credit for ferreting out some answers, but without your direction, we would've handed off the case to the police, and she'd be driving up and down the beach and ticketing people for littering."

"The only people who think they work in a vacuum and deserve all the credit are assholes and the FBI. Rachel and I are a team, and she's doing a good job. She deserves the bulk of the credit."

We walked down the hall. Matt put his hand on my shoulder. "I read Jill's reports on your work in Flagstaff, and then I did an internet search for the wire service articles on your two investigations. You are the most selfless person I've ever met. The newspapers interviewed all the people you worked with, and those other law enforcement officers all heaped praise on you."

I clenched my jaw, not liking where the discussion was going.

"You're not going to comment, Doug?"

"My old football coach painted a quote in the football locker room. It's rumored Ara Parseghian said it first, 'There's no 'I' in team.'"

"You are a GS-14 because someone far above my pay grade thinks you deserve much more credit than you're willing to accept. Based on what I'm seeing, I'm inclined to agree with him. I don't think you know this, but there are only a handful of investigators at your pay grade, and most of them are supervisors in Washington D.C. Whether you like it or not, you're an extraordinary individual in the Park Service."

"I…"

"Doug, you were in the Army, right?"

"Actually, it was the Minnesota National Guard. But, yes, I was in the military."

"What was the correct response when a senior officer told you something?"

"Yes, sir."

"I like what you're doing, and it's okay to accept responsibility for doing a good job."

"Yes, sir."

"Cue up the video and show me what you and Rachel discovered."

"We have to wait until Rachel gets back with the CD and the detective. We have to maintain control of the chain of evidence or some smart defense attorney will get it thrown out in court."

"Good catch. Did you need to remind Rachel about that?"

"She understood what needed to be done."

"After you reminded her?" Matt read my expression. "Don't bother answering. You're doing a great job of training her and reinforcing what she's learned."

Rachel led Dixon into the break room and introduced him to Matt. Dixon watched the video, made some notes, then asked Rachel to put it back into its case. He slipped it into an evidence bag, sealed the bag, and had Rachel sign the chain of evidence.

Dixon added his own signature to the bag. "This has been in your control the entire time since you received it from the gas station, right?"

Matt smiled at me and winked.

"Yes, it has."

"What was that all about? Don't tell me you screwed it up."

"No. It's been in Rachel's control the entire time we've had it."

"What's with the sly look and wink?"

"Doug had to remind me to take it out of the recorder and put it into my pocket when I went out to meet you at the entrance."

"Doug's her training officer," Matt explained.

Dixon smiled and tapped the bag. "This is golden. You guys did a good job."

I smiled. "Rachel did a good job."

Chapter 21

I sat in Matt's office recapping the Kaplan case when his phone rang. He glanced at the caller ID, apparently planning to ignore it, then he put up one finger and pressed the speakerphone button. "Superintendent Mattson, how can I help you?"

"I hate to interrupt you. I actually expected to get a receptionist. This is Frank Smith, from the Emporia PD. I promised you a call about Caitlyn Robinson."

"We're a small operation with no budget for a receptionist. Thanks for calling me back. I'm here with Doug Fletcher, and I just put you on speakerphone. I hope you don't mind."

"Hi, Fletcher. You made the original call to me, right?"

"That was me. What's happening with Cait?"

"Well, it's been interesting. Texas CPS put her on a plane two days ago. I picked her up at the Kansas City airport and delivered Cait to her aunt Melinda, in Prairie Village, Kansas. There was a lot of hugging and crying. Bottom line is that both Cait and her aunt are happy with that arrangement. Cait's starting school there without missing a beat."

Matt leaned close to the speakerphone. "What happened with Cait's mom and stepfather?"

The detective chuckled. "They're quite a pair. I showed up at their door with a pair of patrol officers and a search warrant. I tried to downplay it like I was just letting her know we'd located Cait and she was healthy and safe. Cait's mom opened the door, saw the two uniforms and gasped like she thought we were delivering bad news. I gotta tell you, this was three in the afternoon, and I could smell booze on her breath. She looked like hell in a grease-stained t-shirt and baggy sweatpants. I assured her Cait was okay, and she grabbed the doorframe like she was going to swoon. Then, this guy yells from somewhere behind her, asking who's at the door. She says, 'Cops,' and the guy comes flying to the door like his pants are on fire. I recognized him from the bank."

"Cait's stepfather is a banker?"

"He's their car loan officer. He's got an office in the back, but he's not really one of the bank bigshots. Anyway, he looked at me and the two uniforms and asked, 'What's up?' When I told him we'd located Cait, he just nodded and said, 'that's nice.' He didn't ask where she'd been, if she was okay, or if she was coming home soon. Nothing. So, I asked him to step out of the house for a minute so we could have a word, and he gave me the stink eye. 'Why?' he asked. So, I explained it smelled like his wife has had a couple toots, and maybe he should talk to me about making arrangements for Cait's return. He didn't look happy, but he stepped out and followed me to my car. In the meanwhile, the uniforms handed Cait's mom the search warrant and told her to step inside with them."

"That's usually when the fireworks start."

"Yup. The mom howled and yelled for Harry to get over there. He took a step, and I just put my hand up and told him the guys were picking up clothes for Cait. He nodded, but the mom continued to yell. So, I told him I wanted to talk about changing Cait's living arrangements now that she's back. He cocked his head like he didn't understand what I was saying, then Mom howled, 'That little bitch told the cops you were banging her!'"

"The stepfather looked at me and turned red. So, I asked him if he had anything to say in his defense, and he said he wanted a lawyer. I told him he wasn't under arrest, and that we were just having a little chat. He shook his head. 'Not without my lawyer.' So, I cuffed him, read him the Miranda card, and put him in the back of the car."

"Did your search turn up anything useful?"

"Cait's bedroom was pretty much as she described it. No one had touched a thing while she was gone. Her nightie was on the bed, and there were clothes all over the floor. We darkened the room and brought in a UV light source and half the room glowed. We found

Cait's blood on the sheets and on her nightie, and there was semen all over the place; nightie, sheets, panties, jeans. The state crime lab called this morning and told me there are at least half a dozen DNA profiles in the semen samples we collected. We confronted Mom and her public defender. She spilled the whole story, naming names, and begging us to keep her out of jail. Her expression was almost comical when I explained we weren't talking about jail, but years in prison for everyone involved, including her."

"So, how many arrests have you made?"

"We started out with seven, then the stepfather's poker buddies started turning on each other, and we ended with a dozen arrests. We got the stepfather on rape and solicitation of prostitution, which we expected. What we didn't expect was him scamming the bank with one of the car dealers, taking money under the table for approving loans for subprime customers. That got the attention of the Feds, who are going to arrest him as soon as the state gets through with his trial."

Matt leaned forward. "And the mother?"

"Child endangerment and a plea agreement to serve three years in prison and five years of probation after she testifies against all the men."

I smiled at Matt, nodded and said, "Your chief should be pleased with you. You really did a great job."

"The chief and mayor bought me lunch. That's about as good as it gets in Emporia.

Thanks guys. You didn't need to make the call, but you really helped me put together the pieces."

I added, "This is Fletcher. I used to be a detective before I joined the Park Service. I know how hard the job is sometimes."

"I've got one question for y'all. You know who gave Cait the ride to Texas, don't you?"

"It was some guy named Paul, driving a black Jeep. That's literally all I can tell you."

Matt smiled and shook his head.

"That's your story?"

"It's the truth."

"Well, thanks. Y'all have a good day."

* * *

Rachel sat in my guest chair, gushing about the chain of events we'd set in motion by getting Cait hooked up with the Corpus Christi authorities when my cellphone rang.

"Fletcher, this is Scott Dixon."

"Detective, I'm here with Rachel Randall. I'd like to put you on speakerphone."

"Sure. I wanted to update you. We got a 911 call about a dead body found by a maid in an old motel. The responding officers determined it was an overdose and were going to call to have the body transported to the morgue. A sergeant arrived and put everything on hold when he assessed the scene. He called me because the guy didn't have any needle marks, and he just didn't look like a junkie. I've

251

got to give the sergeant credit. Everything in the room was set up to look like an overdose, but there were just a couple hints it was more than that.

"Bottom line, it was a murder. I just got off the phone with the medical examiner, and she found one needle mark, on the back of the guy's shoulder. No way he could've dosed himself there. The drug was heroin laced with Fentanyl, which is what we found in the spoon by the bed, but there wasn't any envelope of dope. The guy had a rap sheet three pages long, mostly assaults and stupid shit, but lately he's been off the radar, which makes me think he's gotten smart or has someone looking out for him."

"That sounds like good police work. What's that got to do with us?"

"I'm pretty sure he's one of the two guys on the video you and Rachel recovered from the convenience store."

"I don't suppose you found Wendy Kaplan hiding in the closet, or incriminating fingerprints."

"There were no fingerprints, which was another red flag. The whole hotel room and bathroom had been wiped clean. The place didn't have any security cameras, and the manager didn't remember anything about the people who rented room eight, or much of anything since Y2K. So, he was useless. We did get security camera images from the Circle K next door, and it shows a minivan that looks like the same one from your convenience store, but we couldn't see the license or any of the faces."

"So, our pair of killers/kidnappers is now down to one guy, who's somewhere with Wendy Kaplan."

"Wendy Kaplan showed up in the hospital ER. We got a call from the hospital and her father flew in from Wisconsin. She's pretty strung out, but she's in an in-patient treatment facility. I hope they can get her weaned off the heroin and get her some counseling. She doesn't remember most of the time she was strung out, so she hasn't been much help in locating the other kidnapper. She knows her husband is dead, but doesn't know, or remember any of the circumstances."

"I don't suppose you have the second guy in custody?"

"He's in the wind. We don't have his name, a good set of prints, or a clear picture of his face. Wendy has a vague recollection his name was Merle, or something like that, which isn't much to go on."

"Thanks for the update, and good luck tracking down Merle." I hung up the phone.

"At least they found Wendy alive," Rachel said.

"I think that's the best possible outcome. Most kidnapping victims don't live through the experience unless the case is closed within forty-eight hours."

Chapter 22

Jill lounged on the couch reading with one foot tucked under her and an iced tea on the end table. "How did the search for the killers go today?"

"The missing widow showed up in a hospital emergency room suffering from drug withdrawal symptoms. I'd say that's a pretty good day. How about you?"

"I had lunch with Mandy and a friend of hers who's a realtor. The people here are really nice."

"Realtors are paid to be nice."

"It's more than that, Mr. Cynical. Everyone I've met has been welcoming and friendly. Flagstaff was nice, but this place is different. I feel like…I guess it feels like this could be home." Jill reached out to hug me. "Ew. You need a shower." She pushed me away.

* * *

I was toweling off when the doorbell rang, so I quickly dressed. Male voices grabbed my attention as I stepped down the stairs. Jill jumped up and poured iced tea from a pitcher and handed me a glass. Matt and a man wearing an expensive suit and a tasteful tie sat in the living room drinking iced tea.

I reached out my hand to the man in the suit who sat across from Matt Mattson. "I'm Doug Fletcher. I see the FBI has taken over the case."

Matt looked uncomfortable. "Special Agent Jones showed up in my office just after you left. He wanted to update us on the body you and Rachel recovered from the surf."

Jones smiled at Jill, and with a silky Texas twang said, "I wonder if we could have a moment alone with Superintendent Mattson and Ranger Fletcher."

I gestured for Jill to take a seat on the sofa. I pulled a dining room chair to the living room and sat down. Special Agent Jones looked unhappy. "I think Park Service Superintendent Rickowski is entitled to sit in on the discussion. She's been my partner through much of this investigation."

Jones looked at Jill. "Superintendent Rickowski?"

"Jill is the superintendent of the Flagstaff Park Service office. She's visiting Texas on her vacation."

"I'm sorry, Superintendent Rickowski. I didn't realize you were a member of the Park Service."

Jill, in a flowered summer dress and sandals, didn't look like a Park Service superintendent. Being cagey, she smiled. "I imagine FBI agents wear civvies when they're off duty too."

Matt was confused by the discussion but smiled and let me take the lead.

"I assume you've come to announce the FBI has taken over the murder case."

Jones nodded. "We've identified John Doe and found his wife. I came to Superintendent Mattson to get the Park Service's case files. He said you were the lead investigator and told me you'd left for the day. Time is of the essence, so we drove here to speak with you."

"You identified John Doe? I didn't realize the FBI had a medical examiner in Corpus Christi. Or, do you mean the M.E. put John Doe's fingerprints into the IAFIS database, and they were associated with someone of interest, which rang a bell in the FBI offices?"

Jones gave me a withering glare. "We are working with the Nueces County Medical Examiner on the case. The FBI made the identification."

"I see. I take it John Doe is someone important enough to justify the FBI's interest."

"I'm not at liberty to discuss his identity. I came to superintendent Mattson to get your files and the video recording from the gas station."

"Who is John Doe?"

"I just said…"

"I know what you said. I asked who John Doe was, and I'd like to know why you're suddenly interested in the case."

"The investigation is at a very sensitive point, and I'm afraid you don't have a need to know."

"Ah, you're about to have a press conference, and you don't want any of the other involved agencies to leak the information to the media before you can spin it to make the case look like it's yours."

Jones clenched his jaw.

I leaned forward and set down my iced tea. "This isn't my first experience with the FBI, Special Agent Jones. The FBI has taken over cases from me before, often after we've solved them. They've grabbed all the case files, told us nothing, then called a press conference to announce *they'd* solved the case. On rare occasions, they've allowed the police chief to stand in the background during the press conference, but they've only admitted the participation of the other involved agencies under extreme duress."

"This is an interstate kidnapping, Fletcher, and that makes it an FBI case. I'd like to stop wasting our time. I'm politely requesting your file and the video. Don't make me push this up the chain of command. It could get ugly for you."

"I'll gladly hand over my case files. Who is John Doe?"

Jones glared at me. "His name is Theodore Kaplan."

"And why is he important enough to get on the FBI radar?"

"He's a county prosecutor for Hennepin County, in Minnesota."

"There, wasn't that easy. What you don't know, is Ranger Randall and I identified Ted Kaplan yesterday, identified his flight from Minneapolis, and gave that information to the Medical Examiner and Corpus Christi police. We found Kaplan's condo and were there when it was searched by the Corpus Christi police. Ranger Randall recovered the security video from the convenience store with the images of the two men who kidnapped Wendy Kaplan."

"That was good basic police work. Now we need to take your pieces and put them into the greater case file."

"When's the news conference, Jones?"

"We'll make an announcement at an appropriate time."

"Is it tomorrow? I want Ranger Randall on the platform during the news conference, and you'll mention her role in solving the crime."

"Listen, Fletcher, this isn't your case, and it's hardly your place to dictate what's going to happen at the news conference."

I took out my cellphone and chose Sarah Hawkins' *Santa Fe Journal* number from the directory. Everyone watched with curiosity. I prayed Sarah would answer.

"Hi, Doug. What's up?"

"I've got another FBI agent here trying to steal the glory on a case I'm working. Type Corpus Christi, Texas into your computer. Then add Ted Kaplan, K-A-P-L-A-N. We recovered his body from the Gulf of Mexico on Monday."

Jones jumped off the couch and walked over with his hand out. "Who are you speaking to?"

I stepped back, keeping the phone out of his reach. "His wife, Wendy, was kidnapped, and she was just discovered in the Corpus Christi ER, after having been drugged with heroin the past week. The kidnappers used her to lure her husband to Texas."

"What are you talking about?" Sarah asked.

Jones lunged at me and knocked the phone from my hand. He scooped the phone off the floor and stepped away from me. "Who is this?"

"You're not Doug. Who are you?"

"This is FBI Special Agent Mark Jones. I see on the caller ID that you're Sarah Hawkins. What's your interest in the case Ranger Fletcher is pursuing?"

"Janice!" Sarah yelled, trying to get her intern's attention. "Drop everything and get over here!"

Janice rushed into Sarah's cubicle as the phone was switched to speaker mode. "Special Agent Jones. What's going on with Ted Kaplan in Corpus Christi?"

Sarah typed in Google and Ted Kaplan's name. A story immediately popped up about Hennepin County and a prosecutor who failed to appear for the opening comments of a drug smuggling case.

Jones pushed the "off" button on the cellphone and dropped it into his pocket. "That was dumb, Fletcher. You could be charged with interference in a Federal investigation. Who is Sarah Hawkins?"

"She's a reporter with a national byline. I imagine she's already checking on Ted Kaplan, Corpus Christi, and the FBI. If Ranger Randall is on the platform during tomorrow's news conference and getting credit for her role in the solution of the kidnapping, Sarah will have to dig out the story, piece by piece. If you choose to exclude us, Sarah's story will be on the wires before your news conference, and it'll say the Park Service and Corpus Christi police solved a kidnapping and murder."

"Mattson, order him to stand down."

Matt took out his cellphone and dialed a number from its memory. "Chuck, this is Matt Mattson. We've got a joker from the FBI here who's trying to take credit for the work my rangers have done identifying a murder victim and the rescue of his kidnapped wife. Yeah, the one we spoke about this morning." Matt listened while Jones rolled his eyes. "Do you still have a contact at the Washington bureau? Have him call Sarah Hawkins. Who does she work for, Doug?"

"*The Santa Fe Journal*," I replied loud enough to be heard on the phone.

Jill grabbed her phone off the counter and ran through her call history. She chose a number and hit dial. "Hi, this is Jill Rickowski, from the

Flagstaff Park Service office. Please pass a message to the Secretary of the Interior that the FBI is trying to steal the glory for another Park Service investigation. He can reach me at this number to get the details. I'd appreciate it if he'd call the Attorney General before the story hits the wire services again."

Jones threw my phone on the table. It skittered across and bounced off the wall, leaving a mark in the sheetrock. "Screw all of you," he said before storming out.

Matt ended his call and looked at me. "What the hell was that all about?"

"The FBI is very political, and they get press by taking credit for solving high profile crimes. They don't like to admit other agencies participate in the investigations, and they really dislike it when another agency actually solves the crime and gets the story out before they can hold a press conference and claim the glory."

"I see them doing press conferences all the time with a lineup of local officials behind them."

"Have you ever heard them mention the contributions of the other agencies?"

"I don't recall."

"The next time you see an FBI press conference, listen closely. You'll hear them say we, us, and our, often. Rarely, will you hear them say joint investigation or announce the significant contribution of another agency. They can't afford to share the glory, or they won't get brownie points and their next big promotion."

"I have a hard time believing that."

Jill set her phone on the table. "It's true. The FBI refused to investigate Doug's first case and then didn't want him on the podium during the press conference. After Doug gave the case details to the reporter from *The Santa Fe Journal,* the Secretary of the Interior read the wire service article. He called the Attorney General and insisted the FBI include the Park Service in the FBI press conference. They reluctantly allowed Doug on the podium."

My phone chimed, and I had to search on hands and knees before I located it under the sofa. I got it before it rolled over to voicemail. "Sarah?"

"Doug, what's going on? Who was that FBI guy?"

"It's the same old bullshit. My partner and I recovered a body from the surf, and we identified him as a Minneapolis prosecutor. Now the FBI is calling a press conference to announce they've solved the case."

"I got some information from Reuters on Theodore Kaplan's disappearance from Minneapolis. Tell me about your role in this, and I'll get it on the wires in the next hour."

Jill's cellphone vibrated while I was briefing Sarah. "Mr. Secretary, thanks for returning my call. We've got another situation with the FBI, like the case with the antiquities and bodies on the reservation. Doug Fletcher and his Park Service partner recovered a body from the surf on Padre Island National Seashore.

They identified him as a Minneapolis prosecutor whose wife had been kidnapped. They worked with the local police to identify the kidnappers, and they've found the wife at a local hospital. An FBI agent just showed up at our house and demanded Doug's files. It sounds like they're planning a news conference for tomorrow to take credit for solving the case."

Jill listened for a minute. "I know, sir. It's just like the last time. I was hoping you could contact the Attorney General to warn him there will be stories on the wire service shortly that announce the Park Service as the agency which identified the body of Ted Kaplan, the missing Minneapolis prosecutor. Doug, working with the Corpus Christi police, solved the kidnapping of the prosecutor's wife. That will be contrary to what the FBI intends to announce at tomorrow's news conference. We suggested we'd cooperate if they'd put our rangers on the podium during the press conference, but they refused."

Jill handed me the phone. "Mr. Secretary?"

"It sounds like you've got another hot potato, Fletcher."

"Yes, sir."

"Have you contacted the media and supplied them with our version of the story?"

"I was just doing that when you called Superintendent Rickowski. My contact at *The Santa Fe Journal* is working on a story through the wire services for immediate release. It'll be run in their print edition tomorrow."

"Good job. Get out your uniform and spit-shine your shoes. I'll see that you're on the podium with the FBI during the news conference."

"Actually, it was Ranger Rachel Randall who played the key role. She made the phone calls to isolate possible incoming flights, identify the victim, and she found the security tape showing the two men who kidnapped the victim's wife."

"You're still playing humble, Fletcher?"

"No, sir. Rachel Randall deserves the credit for this one."

"Is she working for you?"

"We're a team, sir."

"Listen, Fletcher. Dust off your dress uniform, including the hat you hate to wear. Be at the press conference. That's an order."

"Yes, sir,"

"Give the phone back to Superintendent Rickowski.

Jill listened and responded with "yes, sir," a couple times. "The flood investigation is ongoing. I'm visiting Texas while I'm on leave. Matt Mattson is the Padre Island National Seashore Superintendent, and Doug reports to Matt."

Matt listened to all the discussions and anxiously awaited the results of the call. "Well?"

"The Secretary is calling the Department of Justice and demanding recognition of our contribution to the case. He's leaving a message for the Attorney General and hopes the wire services pick up the story before he gets called back."

Matt was in awe. "Wow! What about Rachel?"

"The Secretary was rather blunt and said he was tired of Fletcher's hiding his role in these investigations. His words, 'Doug is a damned GS-14 investigator, and that's what people at that level should be doing.' He fully expects Doug to be on the platform, in his dress uniform, looking like a Park Service recruiting poster. You're supposed to write a letter of commendation for Rachel's file."

I shook my head. "Shit."

Matt looked dazed. "I've never dealt with the FBI. Having a special agent show up unannounced at your office door is intimidating. I liked the way you handled him, Doug."

Jill went to the refrigerator and took out the bottle of margaritas. She poured herself a glass and drank half of it. "It was a memorable performance. Jamie Ballard said you were pretty hard on the FBI guy from Phoenix. Having seen this discussion in person gives me a whole new perspective on what happened after the FBI got involved in the antiquities investigation." She took another sip of margarita, then added, "You should've seen the look on Jones' face when he realized you were talking to a reporter."

"I needed to turn the tables on that arrogant jerk, and the only play I could think of was to call my contact in Santa Fe. The ball is rolling now. I don't see a lot of point in showing up at the press conference."

I went to the refrigerator and took out two beers and handed one to Matt. He took a long drink. "I don't think you've got a choice, Doug."

"I'm going to be sick tomorrow. I think you and Rachel should fill in."

Matt laughed. "I've never spoken with the Secretary, but I understand he's quite direct and doesn't suffer idiots well. I suggest you make sure your uniform is pressed."

I looked at Jill, who smiled. "Remember my admonition from last time?"

"Yeah. Suck in my gut and make sure my zipper is up."

"I think your stint in school took care of the gut sucking. Just make sure your zipper is up."

Matt laughed and drained his beer.

"I need to call Sarah again and fill in the blanks," I said. "I'm sure she's got more questions."

Jill walked Matt to the door, and I redialed Sarah Hawkins' cellphone.

"Doug? What's going on?"

"The FBI is more than a little pissed because I handed you background on an active investigation. Did you get enough of an outline to pull together a story?"

"Not at all. Janice is pulling together background on Ted Kaplan and the case he was working on, but there's no explanation for his missing the trial, nor is there anything about his wife disappearing."

"My partner, Rachel Randall, and I recovered a body from the Gulf of Mexico. The M.E. speculated the victim had been drinking and eating smoked almonds, so I sent Rachel on a hunt to see who might've been on a one-way first-class ticket to Corpus Christi. She narrowed it down to three people, and Ted Kaplan was the only one missing."

"What are you doing in Corpus Christi?"

"I'm here to track down people dumping toxic waste on Park Service land."

"And this Rachel, she's a Park Service ranger?"

Jill returned and pressed her ear against the phone. I put it on speaker and set it on the table. "Yes, Rachel is a law enforcement ranger assigned to the Padre Island National Seashore."

"Tell me about Kaplan's wife. She was kidnapped?"

"It appears Wendy Kaplan flew down to stay in their Texas condo while Ted was preparing for the trial. We went to their condo and found that she'd been drugged and disappeared in the company of two guys. We just heard from the Corpus Christi PD she'd shown up in the emergency room going through heroin withdrawal."

"I talked to the evening editor at the Minneapolis newspaper and they've got none of this, but he was willing to send me background on the Kaplans in return for a story ahead of the wire service."

"What did he have?"

"Kaplan is an up and comer in the Hennepin County Attorney's office. He and his wife, Wendy, are big on the social scene and Democratic party. There were rumors he was in line for an appointment as a judge or as the next county attorney. It sounds like his non-appearance for a big case threw it into turmoil and almost got it tossed from the docket. I guess there was a lot of maneuvering at the county attorney's office to keep the court date and reassign counsel."

"I assume Kaplan's disappearance and the start of the case aren't a coincidence."

"The editor was totally in the dark. The county attorney's office has withheld comment, so there's been a vacuum. He was delighted to hear from me, although I got the standard question about a connection to New Mexico. I had to tell him I had a reliable source I couldn't identify."

"Thanks, but the FBI already knows I called you, so the cat is out of the proverbial bag."

"Sarah? Hi. This is Jill Rickowski. Don't let Doug sell himself short in this story. He's been prompting Rachel, and she's following his lead."

I grabbed the phone and turned off the speaker function. "Ignore Jill. She's been drinking and hasn't been privy to the full case."

"Is she your boss from Flagstaff?"

"Yes. She's vacationing in Texas."

"Hi, Jill. Can you answer a couple questions?" Jill must have heard Sarah's raised voice and tried to wrestle the phone away from me.

"I had to shut down the speakerphone and Jill's indisposed."

"I am not indisposed!" Jill yelled at the phone. "I'm right next to him, and he's being a jerk!"

"Doug, put her on the phone," Sarah said softly.

I handed the phone to Jill and stepped away, deciding it was time for another beer.

"This is Jill. You're back on speaker."

"How did you happen to be vacationing in Texas when all this broke?"

"I'm staying with Doug while I'm down here."

"What hasn't Doug told me?"

"I think he's filled in everything he knows about the case. There's a Corpus Christi detective named Scott Dixon who can fill in more blanks. And I know Park Service Ranger Rachel Randall would add colorful commentary to the narrative."

Sarah's computer keys clicked. "So, Jill, you're staying with Doug. Is there something to be read into that?"

"No!" I yelled as I unscrewed the cap from a beer bottle.

"I hope so," said Jill.

Sarah laughed. "He seems a little crusty."

"He's nice when you get past the crust."

I grabbed the phone and disconnected the call. "I'm pretty nice when you get past the crust?"

Jill put up her hands. "I just call 'em as I see 'em."

Chapter 23

"I need to burn off some adrenaline. Let's go for a walk on the beach."

"You just opened a beer, and I have shrimp salad in the refrigerator. Let's walk after supper."

"I'm too keyed up to eat. Give me ten minutes to unwind."

Jill took my beer and set it on the counter, then put her arms around my neck. "I have a different idea, and I hope it'll take more than ten minutes." She pressed her body against me and tilted her head back, inviting a kiss. When I didn't respond, she grabbed my butt with both hands and pulled my hips hard against her. "Don't play hard to get. I can tell you're interested."

When I laughed, she poked her thumb into my ribs.

"Ouch! Okay! You're about as subtle as a hurricane."

"Listen, Fletcher. I've been subtle and reserved for a long time. Don't you think it's about time I try for the brass ring when I've got the chance?"

"Brass ring? Most girls are holding out for a diamond."

"I might not turn down a diamond if one was offered."

"Might not?"

"Depends on who's asking and how he asks."

"You seem so relaxed," I said, slipping off my shirt.

Jill ducked into the bathroom. "Do you mean because I have a libido?"

"That, too. But you're just taking life as it comes. You don't seem stressed out about your job situation or uncertainty about the future."

She emerged from the bathroom wrapped in a towel, then modestly shed it once she was under the sheets. "Well, about the libido part. My entire experience with sex was with a narcissistic cowboy, and as far as I knew, only one of us enjoyed the experience. That was followed by thirty years of celibacy. I read about romance in *Cosmopolitan*, but I believed a woman enjoying sex was a fictional concept."

"And then you met me?"

Jill pulled me close and tucked her head alongside my neck. "I have two data points in my sexual history. A selfish cowboy and a gentle cop who treats me with care and respect. I prefer this end of the spectrum. I suppose there might be something better out there, but I'm quite pleased to be here with you."

She pulled my mouth to her and gently kissed me. "And how about you?"

"What about me?"

"Are you happy where we're at? Do you want more?"

"I'm happy, but scared."

She leaned away from me. "What are you afraid of?"

"I'm afraid of what happens when the Flagstaff investigation is over. What happens to us if they call and say you can have your old job back?"

"What do you want to happen?"

"As much as I want you here, I want you to be happy."

"I'm happy."

"You're on vacation. Of course, you're happy. What happens if your Park Service career goes away? Can you be happy here once the vacation is over, and this is what the rest of your life is going to be?"

"I think so. I guess I can't say without living this life for a while, but there's still the question about you. Can you be happy with an older woman built like a tomboy?"

"I think my body is answering that question."

"I need the answer to come from your head, not your crotch."

"The answer is the same for both of them."

She pushed herself onto her elbow and stared into my eyes. "Are you joking around again, or are you serious?"

"If we could never have sex again, I'd still want to lie beside you and hold you close."

"You're serious?"

"I'm serious."

She eased herself back down and put her head on my chest. "I feel like I don't deserve you."

"I'd feel hollow if you left."

Her eyes darted to my face to see if I was smiling, then she put her head on my chest again.

"What happens if you're asked to return to Flagstaff?"

"I...need something permanent in my life. The Park Service is an old comfortable place, and if they take me back, I know I'd be comfortable there. On the other hand, this is the happiest I have ever been. I don't want to leave it behind if we can..."

"If we're in love?"

"Yeah. If we're in love," she said.

"I can only speak for half of us."

"Shh. I'm still having a hard time getting my head around whatever it is we have. I'm afraid calling it love will cheapen it."

I rolled on top of her, smiling. I bent my head down, kissed her, and felt her press her hips against me. "Okay. This is pure lust. I lust after you."

* * *

We chatted about the FBI while eating the shrimp salad, carefully avoiding issues of romance and lust. We were loading the dishwasher when my phone rang.

Rachel sounded agitated. "Doug, I'm totally freaked out. I'd hardly hung up after speaking with Matt, then some woman at *The Santa Fe Journal* called. As soon as I hung up with her, the phone rang again, and some guy claiming to be an FBI agent asked for my Kaplan files. What's going on?"

I explained the visit from the FBI and my call to New Mexico. "What did you tell my friend, Sarah?"

"I basically explained what we'd done after finding the body on the beach. She seemed to know it all anyway, so all I was doing was confirming what she already knew."

"Great! Did she say if she'd spoken with Scott Dixon?"

"Yes. He told her Wendy Kaplan is in a private detox center and is doing well. He also told her the FBI had shown up in his chief's office, and they'd agreed to hand over copies of all their files. So, what happens now?"

"It's out of our hands. The FBI is taking over the case. They're probably holding a news conference tomorrow to announce their accomplishments and to say an arrest is imminent."

"An arrest is imminent? Really?"

"I don't know, but that's what they always say."

"I called Matt. He said you're going to be at the news conference."

"I was ordered to show up. I'd gladly give up my spot if you'd like to stand on the podium behind the FBI."

"Ah, no. I don't own a dress uniform, and I'm not into public appearances. You're welcome to that gig. Thanks just the same."

"I think you need to make the morning dune patrol without me tomorrow, at least until I find out when the FBI is having their news conference."

"No problem. I'll grab one of the interpretive rangers to ride along. They like to get out of the office, and maybe we'll see some turtle hatchlings."

I disconnected the call and looked at the waning sunlight. "There's still time for a quick walk."

* * *

Jill seemed unusually reserved during our beach walk. "You're awfully quiet."

"Do you remember the houses on the canals?"

"They're pretty, and the sunsets over the bay must be great."

"Do you remember when I told you Dad had downsized and kept forty acres for a hobby farm?"

The sudden change in topic caught me off guard. "I remember you talking about your parents living on a hobby farm. I don't recall hearing they'd downsized."

"When I was a kid, they had two sections of ranch land. Dad sold off all but forty acres a couple years ago. He told me he'd set up a trust account for me, but I've never understood exactly what that meant."

"Okay."

"I called yesterday and got the details."

"So, you found out the details of the trust. Then what?"

"Do you remember the yellow house that's still boarded up after the hurricane."

I struggled with another change in topic. "Sure. I think it probably needs a lot of work."

"Mandy and I met with her friend, the realtor. The owners gutted it and had an architect draw up plans for interior rehab, but they balked at the price. I like their plans, so Mandy and I walked through it."

I stopped and faced her. "Honey, I doubt we can afford to buy and rehab the interior of that place on our combined salaries."

She searched my face, waiting for my reaction. "Please tell me I'm not a fool."

"Is there more to the story?"

"Between my savings and the South Dakota account, my bank account balance is close to what they're asking for the shell of the house. The realtor said it's been on the market for months, and the owners might be willing to accept a lowball cash offer. We'd have to take out a loan to pay for the rehab."

"What's the problem?"

Jill's voice lost confidence, and she looked close to tears. "I'm not used to being in a relationship. I'm used to just doing things." She paused. "I want you to see their plans and walk through the house. We'd have to continue living in the townhouse for a couple months while the work gets done, but when the house is done…"

I hugged her and felt the tension ease from her body. "That sounds permanent."

She nodded. "I like it here, and I'd like to put down roots. The realtor said she's available tonight. Do you want to see it?"

I turned and started walking toward the townhouse with my arm around her waist. "Sure."

Jill pulled out her cellphone and called the realtor as we walked. "Hi, Glenda. Are you still available to show us the yellow house tonight?"

Chapter 24

I tucked my gun under the front seat of the Isuzu. Traffic on the highway was light, so we only waited a few seconds at the stoplights before we got to the development on the canals. Most of the construction workers had gone for the day, and the few remaining trucks had out of state license plates, making me think the workers might be living inside the homes as they worked.

I drove to the end of the street as the last twilight lingered over the bay and parked behind an ivory Lexus idling in front of the yellow house. A tall blonde woman, dressed in a western-cut blouse, jeans, and boots got out of the Lexus and met us at the Isuzu's fender.

The realtor shook our hands. "Hi, Jill. You must be Doug. I'm Glenda Miles."

Glenda had a cardboard tube under her arm. She spread blueprints on the trunk of her car. "Here are the drawings the architect put together for the current owners. He updated a lot of the layout and created this open space, including the living room, dining room, and kitchen, all overlooking a lanai facing the canal."

Jill looked at me, hopefully. "Don't you think it looks lovely?"

"It looks great, but what does the inside of the house look like?"

Glenda rolled up the plans, popped her trunk, and handed each of us a large flashlight. "The electricity is off, and the windows are boarded up, so we'll need the flashlights." She led us up the sidewalk and unlocked the front door. "Keep in mind it's been gutted, so there's not a lot to see other than just getting a feel for the size of the space."

The front door opened into a vast, empty space. The sheetrock and insulation had been stripped off, exposing the outer walls. The interior walls were nothing more than rows of two-by-fours with wires strung through them. Overall, it looked like the inside of a partially constructed home waiting for sheetrock, flooring, and cabinets.

I sniffed the air. "What's the sickly-sweet chemical smell."

"The contractors sprayed it down with a mildew and mold inhibitor," Glenda said. "That'll dissipate quickly when the windows get opened, and the contractors start working."

Jill looked at me like a kid awaiting parental approval.

I took her hand and squeezed it. "If you think we can afford it, I think it'll be lovely."

Glenda smiled. "I guess that means I should write up an offer."

Jill nodded.

Glenda walked us outside and locked the door. "I'll call the owners and tell them there will be an offer coming for the amount we discussed."

I started following Glenda to the street, but Jill tugged on my arm. "Come look at the view over the canal."

I put my arm over her shoulder, and she snuggled into my side as we walked between the houses. The sun had set, leaving red, orange, and yellow clouds hovering over the bay. We walked to the short pier in front of the house, sat on the bench and snuggled, watching the ripples reflecting the colors of the sky. A boat creaked as it rubbed against a nearby pier, rolling with the swells coming from the bay.

Jill rested her head against my shoulder. "A penny for your thoughts."

"I've never seen a sunset like this in Flagstaff."

"Flag has its own beauty, but you're right, it's hard to beat this view."

I twisted to look toward the creaking boat. "It's odd, but all the other houses have their boats hoisted out of the water. There's just that one that's rubbing against a rubber bumper making that creaking noise."

"Maybe they're broke after doing hurricane repairs."

"All the other boats look like they're deep enough to go out in the gulf. All I can see of the creaking boat is the top of its motors."

"Stop being a cop and just enjoy the sunset," Jill said with a touch of irritation.

I was curious. "Those guys at that house are working late. Let's go see what they're doing for the neighbors." I took Jill's hand and led her down the edge of the canal. "It's too dark to see if that boat's blue or black, but that's a bass boat like the waste dumper was using."

Jill stopped me at the end of the pier where we could look down at the boat. "When I talked to the marinas, they said there weren't many of these around because they're better suited for inland lakes."

"Let's see what the contractors are doing." I could smell solvents and spray paint through open windows as we approached the back of the house. I pulled Jill to the corner, away from the light spilling from the windows. I peeked around the window frame and saw a man spraying black paint on the labels of stacked pails. He stepped back from the pile, picked up two buckets in each hand and carried them out the back door. I pulled Jill around the corner of the house and watched him haul them to the bass boat.

I led Jill to the street. "Call 911 and ask for backup."

"What are you going to do?"

"I'm going to get my pistol out of the Isuzu and ask him what he intends to do with the pails."

"By yourself?"

I unlocked the Isuzu. "I don't know if Port Aransas can get a cop here before that guy leaves with the boat."

I left Jill standing by the Isuzu, talking to a dispatcher. I edged down the side of the house with my back pressed against the siding, duckwalking under the side windows where light spilled onto the yard. I'd almost reached the back door when it swung open again, and the man stepped out carrying more pails. He went to the boat. I stayed in the shadows and stopped at the pier. He set the buckets in the center of the boat, covered them with a blue tarp, then tied the tarp down with bungee cords.

"I assume the pails contain hazardous waste," I said, stepping onto the pier, holding the Sig at my side and my duty belt in the other hand.

He was a big man, dressed in stained white clothing, like a painting contractor. He wore a baseball cap backward, probably the same guy who'd almost swamped my borrowed boat.

"What's it to you?"

"I'm a park ranger, and you've been dumping your pails on Park Service property. You're under arrest."

"I'm being arrested by a park ranger. You're joking, right?"

I raised my Sig, so it pointed at the gunwale of the boat. "Step out of the boat, put your hands behind your head, then walk slowly backward toward me."

The man smiled. "I don't see any of those things happening. If you want, you can come out here and try to handcuff me, but I don't think that'd be wise."

A siren wailed in the distance. The smile left the man's face, and he looked worried at the prospect of a "real policeman" coming to my aid.

He'd thrown the lines clear and pushed off by the time I was halfway down the pier. I heard the outboard motors cranking, and when I reached the end of the dock, the boat had already drifted ten feet into the canal. I assessed my chances of jumping onto the boat as zero, so I helplessly watched the water in the channel swirl as the propellers started rotating. The man smiled, knowing he'd beaten me. With all of Corpus Christi Bay, the Gulf of Mexico, and the channels behind the barrier islands available as escape routes, I figured the odds of capturing him were nil.

I aimed the Sig at the twin outboard motors and fired five shots into them. The man's eyes grew wide when he saw the muzzle flash and heard the report of the gun. He ducked behind the pails.

A pistol appeared over the capstan, and the man fired blindly in my direction without aiming. I took cover behind a wooden piling. One of his wild shots hit the wood, sending splinters into the air.

"Sonofabitch," I muttered and remembered a policeman's corollary of Murphy's Law: *An un-aimed shot is the one that hits you.* Other bullets whizzed past, and I heard windows breaking behind me. As I'd hoped, my shots damaged something in the motors. They started thumping, and one shrieked before stalling.

The twilight was gone, and the muzzle flashes blinded both of us. I fired more shots at the last spot I'd seen the man. Several rounds sounded like they'd struck the fiberglass boat, which provided the painter virtually no shield. The last shot hit with a distinctive "whump" telling me it struck a pail filled with liquid.

The man peeked around the capstan and fired again just as my eyes had adjusted to the darkness. I fired at his muzzle flashes until I was out of shells, then I took cover, ejected the magazine and slammed a new one into the butt of the gun as bullets buzzed past.

"How long before your boots get soaked with whatever's in the pails?" I yelled as the acrid odor of gas and organic solvents hit my nose. The dying motors moved the boat slowly away from the pier.

Another fusillade of shots flew past as I ducked behind the wooden piling. When the firing paused, I swung around the piling and fired at the pile of buckets. It seemed like I'd only fired a few times when the Sig's slide locked back, indicating I'd emptied the second magazine. I was blinded by the muzzle flash and my ears were ringing when I ducked behind the piling to reload.

"Geez man! Knock that off. This shit is flammable!"

I peeked around the piling. "Shut down your engines before they start a fire."

The words were hardly out of my mouth when I was blinded by the fireball set off by the gas leaking inside the motors, followed by the "woof" of solvents igniting inside the boat. I recoiled from the heat of the blast. I saw the silhouette of the man jump out of the boat followed by splashing that sounded like he was swimming. The siren neared as the pyre of burning gas and solvents reached skyward. The splashing continued, so I returned the Sig to my holster.

"Are you okay?" Jill yelled from somewhere near the house.

I shouted to be heard over the roar of the fire. "I'm on the pier! See if there's a buoy or something we can throw to a guy in the water."

The blue and red flashers of the police cruiser pulsated against the houses as it approached. I heard the officer calling for fire units as I walked to the end of the pier to help the man in the water. A can of solvents on the boat "cooked off" and blew flaming solvent in a plume that made me retreat. Within seconds, more cans exploded, covering the boat and the surface of the water with a sheen of burning chemicals. The man in the water was probably past salvation.

A Port Aransas officer met me in the yard. "What happened?"

"A guy had a load of hazardous waste in a boat. We exchanged gunfire, and then his boat burst into flames."

He looked at the flaming platform, hardly recognizable as a boat. "There was someone on that boat?"

"I think he jumped over, but there's so much burning solvent on the surface of the water, I don't think there's a chance he survived."

Fire sirens started growling a half-mile across the channel as the flashing lights of the fire trucks pulled out of the station near the ferry docks. The vehicles were so far away they seemed to move in slow motion. I wondered if they would arrive before the fire burned out.

The boat listed then slipped low in the water. The motors went under, and as the boat filled with water the cans of waste floated, some tipped, adding more fuel to the flames on the water. Jill stood next to the house holding a rope, apparently realizing there was no rush to get it to me.

I walked across the yard to her. "Are you okay? Some of his shots hit the house."

"I'm fine. I took cover in the garage during the gunfire."

I looked at the rope in her hand then at her face lit by the flickering flames. "We're not going to need that."

She dropped the rope. "Are you okay?"

"I'm fine, but there's going to be a pile of paperwork to fill out."

* * *

I spent the next three hours at the Port Aransas police station. I was questioned by a detective, and later, by the chief who'd been called in from bed. At the end of his interview, the chief said, "I guess we'll get your statement typed up and have you sign it. It doesn't look like there are any witnesses to refute your version of the gunfight."

Chapter 25

Jill led me to the bathroom mirror. I stared at my red face with no eyebrows. My clothes were covered with soot and wood splinters.

Jill leaned on the doorframe, gazing into my eyes in the mirror. "I was scared to death. I heard all the shooting, then I couldn't see you when I got to the yard."

"I was safely behind the wooden piling when he shot."

"You're lucky you weren't any closer to the boat when the pails exploded. As it is, you look like you spent too much time in the sun. I'm sure there'll be comments when you show up for the news conference later this morning."

"Later this morning?"

"It's three o'clock. I have a voicemail message from last night. Matt left orders to have you at the news conference at ten. There's probably one on your phone too."

"Call him and explain I'm not presentable."

"I'm not calling him at three o'clock in the morning to tell him you're not going to show. You're going, even if your burns turn to blisters."

She disappeared and came back with a bottle of Aloe lotion. "Close your eyes. I'm going to smear this on your face and hands. It's going to feel like ice water, but it'll keep the swelling down."

* * *

It took a few minutes to find a parking spot near the Corpus Christi police station. Jill and I walked a few blocks toward the barricades set up where dozens of spectators and reporters had gathered for the news conference. I spotted Matt and Rachel's Smokey Bear hats in the crowd, and we joined Rachel, Matt, and Mandy on the sidewalk across the street from the courthouse.

"Your face is the color of a boiled lobster," Mandy said after hugging Jill. "Matt had a call from the Port Aransas Police Chief at three this morning complaining that one of *his* rangers had been in a gunfight in a residential area. He didn't mention that you'd been burned."

Matt shook his head in apparent resignation. "The night you had us over for supper Jill told Mandy that you didn't always color inside the lines. But shooting a boater and burning up a boatload of toxic waste in a residential waterway is way outside the lines. If not for the Reuters article by Sarah Hawkins, you and I would be posted to the Aleutian Islands National Park."

I looked between Matt and Jill. "What did Sarah write?"

Matt looked surprised. "I thought you'd called her. She had all the details of the toxic waste dumping, the gunfight on the pier, and Wendy Kaplan's escape."

Jill handed me my cellphone. "You're lucky I knew your phone password. I found Sarah's name in your call history."

I snatched the phone from Jill, who looked very pleased with herself. "I'm just trying to stand by my man," she said in her best Tammy Wynette accent.

I turned back to Matt. "I expected you to be berating me about the pages of paperwork you'll have to fill out because I discharged my firearm and spilled toxic waste into the boat channel."

Matt smiled. "Oh, it's not *me* who'll be filling out the paperwork, Inspector Fletcher. Between the yet to be found boat captain, the fire, the toxic spill, the sunken boat — yet to be floated, and discharge of over two dozen rounds from your firearm, *you* are going to be getting writer's cramp."

"What are you going to be doing?"

"Besides getting railed at by the Park Service, the Port Aransas Police Chief, and the Texas Department of Environmental Quality, I'll be making sure you get all the paperwork properly filled out and submitted on time."

Jill smiled like a Cheshire cat. I groaned. "What about Rachel?"

"She wasn't at 'The gunfight on the canal' as the morning news reports are calling it. Her plate was cleared when the FBI picked up her notes and file."

I looked at Rachel, who was also smiling. "I'll be patrolling the beach with no paperwork to fill out with a clear conscience."

Jill tugged at my sleeve. "I think they're getting ready to start the news conference."

Special Agent Jones met me on the steps of the Corpus Christi police station. An array of microphones was erected directly in front of the entrance. Jill stood behind the crowd across the street with Matt, Mandy, and Rachel.

Jones handed me a typewritten, double-spaced page. "Here's the deal, Fletcher, I'm doing all the talking. You're going to stand behind me and hope your sunburn doesn't screw up the camera images. This is the text of my statement. Basically, it says, 'In a joint operation, the Park Service, the Corpus Christi Police, and the FBI solved the murder of Ted Kaplan and the kidnapping of Wendy Kaplan.' If that's not good enough for the Park Service, tough shit." Jones walked to the microphones and prepared to make his statement.

Scott Dixon grabbed my elbow and guided me to the steps behind the FBI agent. "Nice hat, did you steal it from the bear?" He paused, then added, "I don't know who you talked to, or what they said to the FBI, but this is the first time I've ever been on this side of an FBI press conference. It's also the first time I've heard the agent say they received assistance from another agency. I want the name of the Park Service's public relations person. We're going to have the chief hire him."

"I had nothing to do with it."

"Sure. Whatever. Jones said together we solved the murder and kidnapping, but as far as I know, their only contribution was finding an abandoned minivan in the airport parking lot."

"I'm sure an arrest is imminent," I said. "They always say that if they don't have the person in custody."

"By the way, what happened to your face and eyebrows?"

"I fell asleep in the hammock." I searched the faces in the crowd and saw my personal cheering section and had an idea. "I'll be right back."

I wound through the crowd and grabbed Rachel's elbow. "Come with me," I said, pulling her toward the steps.

"Why?"

"You're going to be on television. Toby might cut you some slack about being a cop when he realizes what we accomplished."

We ran up the steps while Special Agent Jones fought the wind to keep his notes from blowing away. He saw us as we passed the microphones and was about to admonish me when the woman coordinating the television coverage steered him to the microphones.

"Ten seconds to airtime." She started a countdown with her fingers. Jones glared at me for one second, then composed himself and straightened his tie.

Rachel whispered as I pulled her onto the step alongside me. "I'm not supposed to be here."

"Shut up and look professional."

Special Agent Jones looked very serious. "Good morning ladies and gentlemen. I'm here to announce the successful conclusion of a joint FBI, National Park Service, and Corpus Christi Police investigation…"

Chapter 26

I set my Smokey Bear hat carefully on the top shelf of the closet next to the Sig, then I climbed the stairs. Jill watched me take off my belt and coat and lay them on the bed.

"Your face looks like it hurts. Would you like me to put more Aloe on it?"

I ignored her question and hit a speed dial number on my cellphone as Jill hung the coat in the closet. "Hi, Mom. I thought I'd check-in and see if you saw the news conference."

Jill looked irritated with me for leaving her question about the Aloe dangling. She went into the bathroom and closed the door while I talked to my mother about her bridge club, then updated her on my Texas move.

I was still on the phone when Jill came out of the bathroom. "Hang on, Mom. She's right here." I pushed the speakerphone button and held the phone in front of Jill.

"Jill?" Mother asked.

"Hello, Mrs. Fletcher. Doug just stuck the phone in my face, and I'm not sure why."

"He's just spent the past ten minutes singing your praises. I told him I was happy he'd found someone like you."

Jill gave me a look that asked what was up. "That was very kind of him."

"You must be quite a woman. He wants me to meet you." Jill's eyes grew wide. "Where do your parents live?"

"They live on a hobby farm outside Spearfish, South Dakota."

"Oh good, you're a Midwesterner, too. I think we have more in common with each other than we do with people on either coast."

Jill looked frantic and pushed the phone toward me.

"Mom, would you like to fly down to Corpus Christi to spend a few days with us?"

"I guess there's nothing here that would keep me from doing that. I don't want to intrude. Could you get me a hotel room?"

"That's nonsense. We've got a two-bedroom townhouse. If it's okay with you, I'll book flights and send you the details."

"Where exactly is Corpus Christi?"

"It's on the Gulf of Mexico, about halfway between Houston and Mexico."

"I've never been to the Gulf Coast before. I think that might be fun."

When I disconnected, Jill glared at me with annoyance. "You're going to fly your mother down and dump her with me while you're working? Are you nuts?"

"She'll only be here a few days. I'll book her flights so she'll be here over a weekend, and we can show her around the area."

"Do you think that's wise," Jill asked, looking skeptical.

"It'll be the acid test."

"Oh, yes. It'll be acid all right." Jill thought about that for a second, then asked, "How so?"

"If I can convince her that I'm in love with you, then maybe I'll be able to convince you, too."

"Is that what this is all about. You think you need some grand gesture to convince me we are an item?"

"I felt like I needed a grand gesture to convince you it's worth your while to make a permanent space for me in your life."

"Permanent?" The twinkle in Jill's eyes and her grin had me more than a little worried. "Undress and climb under the covers." She walked into the bathroom. I laid in bed, wondering what she had in mind.

She walked out of the bathroom, hair damp from the shower and body wrapped in a towel. Her grin was gone, and she looked uneasy. She stopped at the foot of the bed.

"You said I could be a model for a sculptor." She dropped the towel and stood naked at the foot of the bed. She turned slowly, showing me her body, previously kept hidden under the covers. When she'd spun completely around, she scampered into the bed and pulled up the blankets. She pressed herself against me and shivered.

I ran my fingers through her damp hair. "That took courage."

"Not courage, it took trust. Complete trust."

"You weren't sure you could trust me?"

"I don't know how to explain it." She paused.

"I'm at a loss for words."

"That's a first. You can usually stick your foot in your mouth without effort. Maybe you're getting smarter."

I pulled her close and breathed in the scent of her shampoo. "That was a big step."

"People throw around the word love too freely. You told me you loved me, and that was sweet, but I've heard it before from men who had no interest in me beyond a one-night stand. I love you, Doug, but more than that, I trust you. I trusted you wouldn't be repulsed by my tomboy body, and I trust you're not going to break my heart. That's a whole level beyond saying, 'I love you' while we're lying naked in bed."

"I had no idea..."

"Doug," she paused and took a deep breath. "I've had a crush on you since our first dinner at Black Bart's."

"You didn't say anything."

"I had a crush on Harrison Ford in the '80s and didn't say anything to him either."

"I think I'm more approachable than Harrison Ford."

"I didn't think you'd settle for someone like me, but now I know you're something extraordinary—this might be the love I've dreamt about my whole life."

She took a deep breath then said, "I went online last night and looked at Park Service jobs. Matt has an opening for a full-time ranger. When we were at the press conference, I told him I might want it. He said he'd be pleased to have someone with my experience."

"What about your superintendent's job in Flagstaff?"

"I plan to resign."

"I'm speechless. Didn't you think we should talk about that?"

"We're talking about it right now."

"So, Texas is something you plan to make permanent?"

"I'm talking about us, Doug, not Texas."

I pulled her to my chest.

"Your mother is coming, and you told her she could stay in the spare bedroom. Where am I going to sleep while she's here?"

"In *our* bedroom. I'm a big boy. She'll deal with it."

"I don't want her to think I'm…a slut."

"You're far from being a slut, and our living arrangements won't shock her."

"There's a complication."

"You're pregnant?"

She pushed my shoulder. "Don't be silly. That's not even a possibility."

"What then?"

"Mom and Dad want to come down to meet you and see the house on the canal. Dad thought they'd drive down in the pickup with his carpentry tools, then he'd do some of the reconstruction and save me…us some money."

"We'll coordinate the visits, so our parents meet each other."

"Are you sure you want to do that? It might create some…" Jill struggled for a word.

"Some friction?" I asked.

"More like expectations," she said with a smile. I must've paused too long. She added, "We don't need to reinforce their expectations. I mean, I understand you went through a painful divorce and living together is a big step for both of us."

"Do you want expectations?"

Jill laid back on the pillows and closed her eyes, deep in thought. "Actually, I do."

"We could create some excitement."

"You mean more than when my dad sees we're sharing a bedroom?"

"Don't you think your parents already know we're cohabitating?"

"It's one thing to *think* that. It's another to see your unmarried daughter sleeping in a man's bed with her clothing in his closet."

"What would they think if they saw a diamond ring on your finger?"

She looked more worried than hopeful. "Please don't toy with me."

"I'm sure there are jewelers in Corpus Christi that are still open."

"You're serious?"

I didn't trust my voice, so I nodded, pulling her into my arms, kissing her forehead.

"Are you asking me to marry you?"

I nodded.

"I want to hear you say it."

"Do I have to get down on one knee?" She shook her head as a tear trickled from the corner of her eye. "Jill Rickowski, will you marry me?"

"Yes." She wiped away the tear with the heel of her hand, then she laid her head on my chest. "I don't want a big rock that gets snagged on everything. Do you think we can find something understated? Maybe a couple small stones set in a simple gold ring."

"It'll be whatever you choose."

"Can we shop for it today?"

"Are you afraid I'll change my mind?"

"All my college friends got their engagement rings thirty years ago. I guess I don't want to wait another day."

I took the Isuzu keys off the nightstand and held them out to her. "Do you want to drive?"

She grabbed her smartphone off the nightstand. "You drive. I'll find a jeweler and navigate."

"Are you going to call your mother?" I asked as we got dressed.

"I'm going to text her a picture of the ring on my finger and wait for her call."

The End

Dean L. Hovey books also published by BWL Publishing Inc.

Stolen Past – Doug Fletcher Book 1

Washed Away – Doug Fletcher Book 2

Dean Hovey is an award-winning author of two previous Doug Fletcher books and nine mysteries set in Minnesota. Dean uses travel and his background as a scientist to add depth to his characters, and authenticity to his locations and plots. He and his wife split their time between Arizona and northern Minnesota.

BWL Publishing

bwlpublishing.ca

Made in the USA
Middletown, DE
09 September 2024